BREAKING BULLETS

MICAH REED BOOK 4

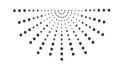

JIM HESKETT

Gonna lay down my sword and shield
  Down by the riverside
  I ain't gonna study war no more
  Study war no more
  Ain't gonna study war no more

— TRADITIONAL

PROLOGUE

Micah Reed let a breath creep from his mouth as he dropped the notebook pages on the table. His lungs deflated, and an odd mix of terror and relief tickled his spine.

In his condo's dining room, across from Micah, Frank Mueller sat, arms crossed and toothpick jutting from his lips. Frank wore a neutral expression, eyes even and mouth flat. He'd been sporting this poker face for the last hour or so as Micah had described every terrible thing he'd done in his life.

Frank now knew more about Micah than any human being alive.

"Anything else?" Frank said.

Micah glanced at the pages on the table. Frayed edges, sloppily handwritten, torn from a notebook.

Eight pages in total with columns and rows. The entirety of Micah's written fourth step in Alcoholics Anonymous; his transcription of his life, including his resentments, his harms to others, his fears, and the inventory of his sex conduct. The written account he had barfed all over Frank to begin the process of leaving the past in the past.

"I don't think so," Micah said, his voice wispy and tenuous.

"It can be overwhelming. Feel like you've had the stuffing knocked out of you, and you could sleep for a week, right?"

Micah nodded. "But it's good, too. I've been so knee-deep in this garbage while I've been getting it all out on paper. Was hard not to wallow in it."

Frank pointed at the pages on the table. "This is who you used to be, kid." Frank raised the finger, leveled at Micah's chest. "And this is who you are now. You stay sober, and you get to leave all that crap in the past. Clean slate."

"I like the sound of that."

"You barely said anything about the end of your time in Oklahoma."

"I told you about Pug," Micah said. "And about Gus and Ramón, and the things we did. What else do you want to know?"

"Have you told anyone how you came to live in Denver? The full story?"

Micah stood up from the table and wandered into the kitchen. His hand shook a little as he poured a glass of water. *The whole story.* He willed his tremors to cease, but couldn't help the way his heart raced.

Micah returned to the table and sipped his water. "No, I've never told the story. The whole thing. A few people have heard bits and pieces. You know more than most."

Frank plucked the toothpick from his lips and folded his wrinkled hands across his belly. His kind face held no judgement, and for that, Micah felt grateful. "It's time to get it all off your chest. Not only the specifics about who you hurt and your part in it, but the whole enchilada."

"It's a lot."

Frank checked his watch. "We got time."

"Some of these details I thought I was going to take to my grave, you know?"

"That's exactly why you need to tell it. Let go of your secrets."

Micah sucked in a breath. "I signed documents and affidavits and all that junk. Now that I've dropped out of the program, I don't know for sure if any of that applies anymore. They always told me that I'm not supposed to tell anyone about what happened to me before I became Micah Reed."

"Too late for that," Frank said, flicking his chin at the stack of papers on the desk. "I know you were born with the name Michael McBriar. I know what you did for a living in Oklahoma, and who you used to work for. Now it's time to connect the dots and let all that crap go, once and for all. Push it out into the room, and then we leave it here, forever."

Micah shuffled the pages, then stacked them back together. His hands wanted to fidget, but he didn't know why. Frank was his AA sponsor and the most understanding person he'd ever known. But Micah knew he would have to utter things out loud that would feel like shoving a knife into his gut. Terrible, unspeakable things.

"I don't know where to start."

Frank coughed, a wet gurgle. "The beginning is always a good place. Or, in this case, the beginning of the end."

"I guess you could say the beginning of the end started with a girl."

Frank chuckled. "Seems like that's a common occurrence for you."

"No, not like that. A young girl, only ten or eleven years old. The day I met her is when everything changed. When the slide into the shit-storm began."

Micah paused, thinking about the day he and Pug raided that house in Mannford. The junkie he'd beaten into a bloody pulp, for reasons that had seemed entirely rational at the time. The violence and insanity that followed.

"And," Micah said, "it all ended with a different little girl."

PART I

THE BEGINNING OF THE END

CHAPTER ONE

AS THE CHEESE fries bubbled up from my stomach and barged into my throat, I barely managed to open the passenger door of the car to lean out in time. A full plate of fries, about a six-pack of beer, and two bourbon chasers ejected from my mouth onto the side of the road in three waves.

"Gross," Pug said from the driver's seat. "If you got any of that on the side of my car, I will never forgive you."

I spit a few times until I'd cleared out the sour wince at the back of my throat. Sat upright in the seat and closed the door. "I know what I'm doing. Didn't spatter at all."

Pug giggled. "You crazy bastard."

I wiped my mouth and yanked the flask from my

pocket, then washed out the terrible taste of puke. "You know it."

"I guess it's a good thing you didn't have to drive here today."

After replacing the flask, I popped open the glove box and removed my new Beretta 92FS. "I don't drive drunk. You know this."

"It's funny that you don't see the irony there, since you're a driver, and you seem to always have that flask with you."

I pivoted in the seat and faced him. "You've gotten sassy ever since you came out."

Pug reached under his seat and fished around until he found his Desert Eagle. He ejected the clip, tapped a finger on the bullet at the top, then popped it back in. "I've always been sassy. You just weren't paying attention."

Pug smiled, but he didn't sell it well. Maybe it was because we were in Mannford, Oklahoma, smack in the middle of red dirt meth country. Or maybe because we were about to walk into some tweaker's house and wave our guns in his face. And we didn't know if the tweaker would be alone, or if he might have a dozen armed tweaker friends with him.

"I don't see anyone scoping us out through the windows," I said.

"Doesn't mean they're not there, Mikey." Now Pug openly frowned. It pulled his face down, making it more angular. Despite the name *Pug*, he wasn't what you might picture: portly with a goatee and natty hair. No, Phillip Gillespie was tall, square-jawed, muscular, with styled blond hair and crystalline blue eyes. I had no trouble believing he was gay when he'd come out. Straight guys don't take such immaculate care of their skin.

Other people in our organization, though, didn't receive the news so well. Of the ones he'd told, at least. Some of them might not hesitate to put a bullet in him if they learned Pug was a *maricón*.

"We can do front-back," I said, "but someone walking in solo might not send the message we're looking for. Depends on if we want show-of-force or kinder-gentler."

"I vote force. Both front, guns out."

I sipped from my flask and slipped it back in my pocket. "Swinging dicks it is, then. Peeing your pants does wonders to make you humble, and I don't think it'll take much to get the message across to this guy."

Pug watched me drink, sighing. "Maybe you could wait until after we do this before having any more?"

"I'm fine," I said. "Cleared out all the space I need. Practically reset me to zero."

Pug rolled his eyes. "What are you, some frat boy? Puke and rally? You're a little old for that."

I studied him, trying to figure out if he was genuinely warning me, or if he was only messing with me. No doubt that he was nervous about what we were here to do.

"Don't worry about me," I said. "I'm good to go."

Pug traced his finger around the steering wheel of the car, and for some reason, the silence bothered me. Grasshoppers clicked and birds chirped, but the void inside Pug's car was louder than a jet engine.

I'd had a sentence on my lips all day, but I hadn't been able to spit it out. The recurring mantra that had been at the front of my brain for the last year or so, every time I slipped a gun into an ankle holster or hid a package behind my Jeep's spare tire.

"I don't want to be here," I said.

"Me neither. Too many unknowns."

"No, I mean at all. I've been giving it a lot of thought lately. I don't want to work for these people anymore."

Pug considered this. "I hear you. It's not like it used to be."

"You have a reason to be here, at least. I don't know what I'm doing here anymore."

We sat in silence for a few seconds, and my fingers drifted down to the bump in my right pocket, where the severed head of a Boba Fett action figure sat next to my car keys. Touching that little piece of plastic gave me some comfort and helped settle my racing thoughts.

Boba and I would chat later when we were alone.

"Let's go," I said. "The longer we sit here, the more likely we are to be spotted."

Pug shoved his Desert Eagle in the front of his pants and cracked open the car door. Let out a dramatic sigh that lasted for at least five seconds. Finally, he plucked the cigarette from behind his ear and stuck it between his lips. "I'm ready to get this over with."

We approached the house at the top of the hill slowly, paying attention to the windows. I didn't see bloodshot eyes peeking out, but Pug was right, they could still be there. Hiding on top of the roof, maybe, or under some of the trash in the yard. You never knew with these crazy rednecks.

But our contact had to have expected we'd be coming. This tweaker had been fronted two ounces of cocaine and had returned zero dollars for our organization's investment. He should have known our employers wouldn't forget about something like that.

The house was ranch-style, one long rectangular structure, like a trailer. Small shed off to the side, and three cars in the yard like abandoned islands. Not up on blocks, but the rusting underneath the cars indicated they'd been marinating there for a while.

I flicked my head at the shed and Pug nodded. He crept up next to one of the cars and sat against the tire, then lifted his pistol at the shed.

With my gun out, I crept toward the little wooden building, then creaked the door open. Nothing but a detached garage filled with tools and car parts. Some remote controls with their guts hanging out, pieces of lawnmowers strewn about the floor. A tweaker's collection of endless projects that had been started but no one would ever finish. Some of those tools might be worth something. I made a mental note, in case this visit went bad.

Sweat dripped from my eyebrow onto my nose, and I wiped it with the sleeve of my t-shirt. July in Oklahoma was brutal like nothing you've ever seen, except for maybe August in Oklahoma. Mosquitos, chiggers, endless breaths of sneeze-inducing ragweed, summer storms with warm rain. I'd had about enough of this place.

For some reason, a canister of bug spray caught my eye, and I lifted it from the shelf and wiped the dust from it. In eighth grade, we used to spray this stuff on hand towels and then inhale the fumes. Crazy, crazy shit we used to do back then.

"You okay?" Pug said.

I spun to find him standing in the doorway of the shed, his pistol at his side.

I lifted the bug spray. "Remember when we used to huff this crap?"

"Do I remember being young and dumb? Most definitely." He beckoned me out of the shed with a flick of his wrist. "Come on. Let's drive down memory lane later. We have work to do now."

I dropped the can of bug spray, and we skulked

toward the house. We paused on either side of the front door.

"Want me to do this?" he said.

"I got it," I said as I raised my leg to kick in the door.

"Wait," Pug said.

I paused. "What?"

"Today's not our day."

I grinned and shook my head. "No, it's not. We'll have more after this."

My leg thrust out and kicked in the door.

CHAPTER TWO

AS I KICKED down the door to the tweaker's house, my nostrils were immediately assaulted by a mixture of cigarette smoke, sweat, and some stinging, chemical smell. Meth cooking, for sure. That acidic tang in the air is unmistakable.

But instead of a house filled with a dozen armed people ready to defend their territory, Pug and I instead found an unoccupied living room. Brown couch marked with cigarette burns and splotchy stains. TV trays folded next to the couch. Green carpet underneath, and a television blaring a dead blue screen, casting a sad glow over the room.

"Listen," Pug whispered, and turned his ear toward a hallway ahead of us. He still held that unlit cigarette between his lips, like a kid with a lollipop. His mouth creased around the cigarette as his neck craned.

I didn't hear anything.

He raised his gun and proceeded into the depths of the house. I followed and pivoted right, checking out the kitchen. Beakers and tubes and half-melted coke cans. Baking trays lined with something that looked like broken glass. The remnants of a small-time meth cooking lab. Not sure why this guy needed to cook, since he'd had two ounces of our cocaine to play with. Maybe he'd sold it all to fund this little home cooking experiment.

If that turned out to be true, my employers would string this tweaker up by his thumbs and bleed him like a pig. That wasn't my problem, though. Pug and I were only here to find out what had happened. If there were a punishment to be doled out, that wouldn't be our job.

Pug glanced at the amateur meth lab and muttered something under his breath. I couldn't be sure, but his lips seemed to be mouthing *white trash*.

"Watch out for needles," he said, keeping his voice low.

He tilted his head toward the hallway, and I raised my Beretta in that direction. My finger kept bumping against the safety, which was starting to annoy me. This was a new gun for me, and I hadn't spent enough time to become comfortable with it. Some guys say a gun is like a lover you have to learn how to touch in the right way, but that's dumb. I'd never found anything so romantic or sexy about a portable killing machine. For me, a new pistol was more like a new car; the clutch and steering wheel feel weird at first, then acceptable, then natural.

Pug's feet shuffled through the dirty carpet in the hallway, and I kept an even pace with him.

Down the hallway were three doors. One straight ahead, which was open, into a bathroom. Then one on each side, both of them closed.

Pug pointed at his chest and then to the right door. I headed for the left one. We reached out for our respective doorknobs, paused for a three count, and then opened them at the same time.

I jumped forward into the room and didn't see anything but darkness at first. The windows had been completely blocked with blankets or newspaper or something, and I needed a second to adjust.

When I could see, what materialized in front of me defied explanation.

Our tweaker, sitting on the floor next to a bed, had his back straight against the frame. Spoon bent over backward on itself in front of him on the carpet, puddle of burned brown liquid in the spoon. A collection of baggies, spent needles, and surgical tubing spread out around him.

In his hand, he held a syringe, his finger in the action of depressing the plunger. But it wasn't his own arm he was injecting with the brown liquid inside. The syringe was sticking out of the arm of a girl, wearing only panties, no top. Her breasts were small, her nipples like droplets of pink on pale white skin. Her stomach flat, her waist tiny.

Very tiny, like some waify supermodel, but she seemed too short for that.

Then I saw her face.

The scene came into focus at once as I connected all of these disparate elements. I realized this girl was so tiny because she couldn't have been more than ten years old. Our tweaker was injecting heroin or another substance into a little girl.

On the floor next to the spoon sat an unrolled condom. A used condom.

I stared at her face, eyes rolling back in her head as the heroin took hold. And then the tweaker's face, grinning at the girl he was injecting. He gazed at her with wanton lust in his glassy eyes.

My mind went blank. I reacted.

The tweaker hadn't noticed me yet, lost in his pedophile fantasy. I raised the gun and swiped the barrel down toward his head, smashing his nose. I heard it crackle and shatter under the force of my pistol-whip.

His hands rushed to his face, and as I raised the gun to hit him again, I noted the girl's head nod back and her body slump to the floor.

I hit him. And again. Blood cascaded down his cheeks as I turned his nose into pulp. Nothing ran through my mind other than a mad desire to keep smashing him until he had no features left.

"Stop!" he screamed. "Please stop."

I couldn't speak. I had no words, and it wouldn't have mattered. My teeth were clenched too tightly. Who could do this to a child?

I kept smacking him, even after he'd sunk to the carpet, his hands feebly swatting at my blows and trying to protect his head. Bones in his wrist broke as I brought the gun down on him again and again.

A hand gripped my shoulder and instinct told me to spin around and shoot, but then I heard Pug say, "Michael, that's enough."

A wave of realization settled over me. I felt the pistol in my hand, the aching tension in my clenched jaw. My chest was shuddering, heart pounding. I became aware of all these things at once.

Pug stood behind me. The tweaker writhed on the floor, his face and neck and t-shirt awash with blood. The girl had sprawled flat on her back, her naked chest rising and falling.

"Jesus Christ," Pug said. "What the hell happened here? Is this what I think it is?"

My hand vibrated in the air, my arm up and poised to strike again. The tweaker fell onto his stomach and crawled toward me. He grabbed me by the ankles and lifted his head, tears now diluting the blood on his face.

"I'm sorry," he said in a muted rasp. "I'm so sorry. Please don't hurt me."

Hearing him speak made me want to pistol whip him again, but our conversation stopped when the girl puked, spewing chunks into the air to splat on her face. Her eyes fluttered, barely open.

I kicked the tweaker out of the way as Pug and I rushed to the girl and turned her on her side. I pushed her chin down with my thumb, checking to make sure she wasn't going to choke on her own vomit.

"What do we do?" Pug said as her hands wrapped around his waist.

She retched a couple more times as Pug patted her back. The girl trembled against him, but she didn't utter a word. She was alive and breathing, at least.

I stood, feeling wobbly. With no food in my stomach anymore and only a few sips of bourbon to calm my nerves, I had to widen my stance to keep from collapsing.

"You," I said to the tweaker. He scooted back against the bed frame, hands up in front of his face. Blubbering. I had to resist the urge to hit him again. I wanted this tweaker dead. I'd never killed a human before, but I wanted to end this scumbag's life more than anything. The intensity of the feeling made my breath catch in my throat. Terrifying and exhilarating at the same time.

"You've stolen two ounces of white from the Sinaloa," I said. "There's only one reason you're still alive." I paused, turned my head to look at the girl. "Our employers want their money, and they've instructed me to give you a chance to redeem yourself. Do you hear me?"

He raised up on his knees, and I got the full sense of what I'd done to him. His nose was broken so badly that it seemed to be sideways on his face. Both of his eyes were puffy and turning black. He spat a tooth on the carpet, sobbing. "I understand."

"And that's for them. For me," I said as I nodded back to the girl, who was now mutely sitting up, with her arms clinging around Pug's waist, "if I come back here, and you're anywhere close to another underage girl, I'll cut your goddamn dick off. You understand that part too?"

He nodded and swiped a dirty hand under his nose.

I shoved the Beretta in my waistband and withdrew my flask. Gulped a deep swallow, letting the burn coat my dry mouth and fill my stomach. I wanted more. I wanted to drink until I could neutralize this unholy anger coursing through my veins.

Instead, I searched around the room for the girl's clothes, then I tossed them to Pug. "We can drop her off at a hospital."

I knelt in front of the tweaker. "And we'll be back in two weeks for the money, the drugs, or your prick on a dinner plate. If you think I'm joking, just wait and see."

CHAPTER THREE

BY THE TIME Pug had driven us back to Oklahoma City, I was drunk enough that I'd stopped seeing the underage girl's nipples every time I closed my eyes. Stopped imposing my sister's face over that girl's face. I don't know why I was doing that, because my sister was ten or twelve years older than that girl. But I couldn't help it. Even at twenty-six years old, I sometimes couldn't get over feeling thirteen, playing with my kid sister at Haikey Creek Park after school.

"Wanna talk about it?" Pug said as we drove along Lincoln, past the capitol building. He slowed to turn onto Culbertson, and I drained the rest of my flask, then let it fall to the floor of Pug's car. Like dropping the mic.

"Not really. I don't even like kids."

"What a nightmare. That whole thing was such a big

mess, you know? We shouldn't have been there alone. We should have had backup, or at least some kind of warning."

"That asshole Ramón," I said as I swiped the flask from the floor and stashed it in my pocket. As I did, I realized my knuckles were covered in blood. Hadn't even noticed it until then. I'd have to take my Beretta apart and clean that, too. I didn't want to think about that pedophile's tainted blood hiding in the crevices of my pistol.

Pug eased into the parking lot of the Freedom House, the old apartment building converted into a drug and alcohol rehabilitation halfway house. At least, two of its four floors were for that purpose. Kinda ironic, when you think about it. The first two floors of the complex were populated with people trying to get off drugs, and they had no idea that the upper two floors were filled with people organizing and weighing the shit right above their sleeping heads.

At least, most of them had no idea. Sometimes, they looked at us funny, coming and going. I had to assume that the program manager gave an orientation to new residents of the house to warn them to stay away from us.

The building was made of brick the color of uneven rust, drafty windows, and rickety fire escapes. The kind of place where you expected nicotine stains to line the edges of pictures hung on the walls. Take a picture down, find a rectangle of lighter-colored paint underneath.

I kept a room on the top floor of this aging brick box, but I didn't actually live here. I still maintained my little apartment behind the plasma clinic in Stillwater, where I'd been living since I'd dropped out of college. Why hadn't I moved to Oklahoma City? Not sure. Something about the college town still called to me, even though I had no stake in it anymore. Call me a romantic for my love of Eskimo Joe's cheese fries and an endless stream of breathtaking twenty-year-old coeds.

Gustavo Salazar and Ramón Frederico ran the operation at Freedom House, a hub for the cartel's Oklahoma City dealings. The whole I-35 corridor operation ran out of this building, actually. From north of Dallas to all the way to Wichita. From Kansas up and from Dallas down were someone else's problem.

Pug parked the car. "What do you figure Ramón's heard?"

"No idea," I said, shrugging. "Everything, probably. You think he's going to be mad about this?"

"I mean, you did smash in the face of his main distributor in Creek County. I'm not saying that pedophile didn't deserve it, but you know how he is. Ramón isn't usually jumping to take our side in stuff like this."

I removed my Beretta from the glove box and

shoved it in the back of my waistband. My head had been swimming for a half hour, and I needed a nap. "Can't do anything about that now. What's done is done, my dear friend Pugsley."

Pug nodded. "Wiser words never spoken, my dear friend Michael."

I socked him in the arm and slipped a box of mints from my pocket. I caught Pug eyeing me as I munched a few of them. A hint of a frown darkened his face. Ramón wouldn't be happy if he found out I'd been drinking today, but I was level enough. I could pass for sober, as long as they didn't smell it on me. Ramón probably assumed I had a raging spearmint habit.

We left the car and strolled across the parking lot. Normally, we'd sneak in the back door through the kitchen, because we weren't supposed to bother the halfway house residents without a good reason. At the very least, they weren't supposed to see any gangster shit going down if we could help it.

But, I didn't feel like skulking around the back, so we walked in the front door. We passed the office of the halfway house manager, some guy whose name I couldn't ever remember. We hadn't been introduced, of course. I was one of the building owner's business associates, and he was a man who was allowed to operate his sober living community for dirt cheap, as long as he didn't ask too many questions.

We strutted down the carpeted hall to the back stairwell and hopped up the stairs. I had to pause between 3 and 4, as the day's drinking and lack of food had caught up with me.

"You have anything to snack on in your room?" I said.

"Yeah, but we should go see him first. He'll know we're here."

"Okay. Let's get this over with." I sucked in a full breath and rambled up the last flight of stairs. Put on my sober face and opened the door onto the fourth floor. Ramón's apartment door stood ajar, first one on the left.

Pug and I shared a look as we removed our pistols and set them on the carpet next to Ramón's door. He was the only person allowed to have guns in his apartment. And he had enough for an army.

I stepped inside to the haze of weed smoke thick enough that I had to squint to see anything. Weed hadn't ever been my preference, but I'd smoked it every now and again, usually when I was too drunk to remember that I didn't like it. Those nights often ended with me getting the spins and puking my guts out.

I seemed to have a hard time learning my lesson with that one.

Some cheerful Mexican trumpet-y music squeaked from tinny speakers in a back room. I could also smell and hear something frying in the kitchen. On the coffee table sat a mirror with five fat lines of white powder, next to a razor blade and a straw. I didn't touch that stuff, at least. Even though I was around it on a daily basis and I definitely could have, I had no desire to become a cocaine casualty.

A moment later, a figure appeared through the haze, which I could now tell was only partially weed, and partially kitchen smoke. Ramón emerged into the living room, wearing nothing but boxers and a bathrobe draped around his potbellied frame. Stomach jutting out like the Buddha. In one hand he held a joint, in the other, a frying pan. He gripped the pan flaccidly, a few droplets of grease randomly plummeting from it to sizzle to their deaths on the carpet.

He and Pug shared a look. Ramón had never liked Pug, for reasons I couldn't explain, and Pug hadn't ever mentioned. Pug was a model employee.

"You two," Ramón said as he took a big pull on his joint. He pointed at the couch in the living room. "Sit."

Pug and I did as we were told.

He stopped a few feet short of us and ground out the joint in the frying pan. Ash from the joint floated through the air and settled into the carpet. "I changed my mind. Stand up."

We rose to our feet.

"You went to Mannford today?" Ramón said.

Pug and I both nodded, even though I assumed Ramón already had heard the story from someone. This was the *toying-with-us* part of the punishment phase.

"And did things go well in Mannford? Did he have the money?"

"Come on," I said. "You know he didn't."

Ramón kept his eyes on Pug as he said, "I wasn't talking to you."

"No," Pug said. "He didn't have the money."

Ramón looked at the frying pan for a second, then he dropped it on the carpet. He raised a hand and smacked Pug across the face. The crack echoed like a rubber band snap in the small apartment.

"Stop," I said, but Ramón didn't listen. He back-handed Pug again.

"It wasn't him," I said. "It was me. I beat up that tweaker."

Ramón glared at me. "Shut your mouth, McBriar. I'm not talking to you."

Pug wiped a spot of blood from his chin. "I'm sorry, Ramón."

"You're sorry. I put you in charge," Ramón said, then he pointed at me. "When you're in charge, and the people you're in charge of mess up like this, that means it's your mess up. You're supposed to communicate."

Pug nodded as he averted his eyes.

I wanted to tell him about the heroin, the naked underage girl, but none of that would matter. Ramón would see only the financial implications. I'd ruined the face of one of his best coke dealers, and so we had to be taught a lesson.

"So what are we going to do about this?" Ramón said.

I spoke up before Pug could accept any more of the blame. "He'll be fine. I bruised up his face a little bit. He's still got hands, so he can sling powder. He knows he has to come up with the money in two weeks."

The words coming out of my mouth made me feel sick. How had my life come to this?

Ramón chewed on his lower lip for a moment and then sighed, seemingly content with my solution. "Okay, fine."

"What about us?" Pug said, his lips trembling.

Ramón glanced down at his hand, his knuckles already turning red. "Both of you, out of here. I don't want to see you for the rest of the day."

"Of course, Ramón," Pug said. "If that's what you want."

I wished Pug would say something; to lash out at this malevolent bastard Ramón. If I did it, Ramón would only smack Pug again. If Pug said something, at least he would earn the beating from Ramón.

But I knew Pug wouldn't do it. He shouldn't do it.

Lashing out and acting impulsively was *my* job.

CHAPTER FOUR

I NAPPED FOR a few hours in the apartment they kept for me on the fourth floor, until I'd sobered up enough to drive. The apartment had exactly these items: a bed with bedding and one pillow, two chairs in the living room, and a handle of tequila in the kitchen, for emergencies. You can see why I didn't like to stay there.

Pug had already left, so I sneaked out the back, ensuring Ramón wouldn't see me. He was still in his apartment, plotting, smoking, snorting.

Pug and I hadn't discussed the discipline doled out in Ramón's apartment. It wouldn't have made any difference if I'd tried to raise the issue. Everything that had gone down in Mannford had been my fault, but I wouldn't have been able to persuade Pug otherwise. He could be a stubborn, altruistic jerk like that sometimes.

Back in my Jeep, I only wanted to escape OKC for a little while.

Oklahoma City is smack in the middle of the state, and I lived an hour north, in the little college town of Stillwater. I had a shoebox-sized one bedroom apartment behind the plasma donation center, between Ramsey and Washington. Not even one bedroom, really, more like one room with a divider. Two story building, and I had the top floor to myself. The bottom apartment was some grad student/weed dealer I'd barely spoken to.

I made an insane amount of money working for the Sinaloa cartel, but it never seemed to stick around. Guys my age were moving out of apartments and spending their paychecks on down payments for houses. Getting married, getting promoted, sharing pictures of their spouses' baby bumps online.

Whatever. I didn't care about the apartment. It was just a place to sleep and keep my beer cold.

I drove up into Stillwater, procured some liquor, and escaped out west of town to Lake Carl Blackwell. Tonight, I would sit by the water, drink myself smart, and figure out what the hell I was going to do about Ramón. Being under his employ was an untenable situation.

I found an isolated spot next to the water, just off the road. The lake had sufficiently twisty trails and enough tree-shrouded picnic spots that I didn't worry too much about someone else coming along to spoil my fun. Stillwater was a college town usually thick with people, but in the summers, it reverted into a little blue-collar map dot like all the others littering the landscape in Oklahoma.

I parked my Jeep and rolled back the top, then reclined the seat and popped open a fifth of Evan Williams. Tossed the cap in the back seat. Didn't matter if I could find it later or not.

I unfocused my eyes and watched the stars cut through the darkness above. Maybe that was why I still lived in Stillwater. Couldn't see the stars in the city, but out here, they were like a million holes in black construction paper. I let my eyes wander until I found Orion in the lower part of the sky, lifted a finger, and pointed at him. He didn't point back.

I dug into my pocket and set the head of the Boba Fett action figure on my dashboard, then turned him so the front of his helmet faced me.

"Big mess today, Boba."

Sure was, Mike, Boba said. *Understandable, though. That piece of shit needed to learn a lesson.*

"That's exactly what I'm saying. You don't mess around with kids. That girl's probably going to need therapy for the rest of her life."

She'll be fine, Boba said.

"You think so?"

I do.

"Shit like that scars a person, doesn't it?"

I have no idea. But what about you? Will you be fine?

I tilted the bottle back and swallowed a quarter of it in three quick gulps. It burned, but after another gulp or two, I wouldn't feel a thing. "Will I be fine? Great question, Boba."

Boba Fett had no reply, so I drank in silence for a few minutes. After another couple deep swallows, I was three-quarters of the way to drunk city. Exactly where I wanted to be. Sleep under the stars with an empty head, and leave my troubles for tomorrow.

My eyelids had grown heavy when I heard something grinding the gravel on the trail not too far from my Jeep.

And then, spoiling the buzz I was working so hard to earn, a pair of headlights reflected off the window. And when I angled the rearview for a better look, the blue and red lights flicked on.

I raised the seat-back and slid the bottle between the center console and the seat. I knew the drill. The car keys weren't in my pocket. I'd stashed them back on the other side of the road so the cop couldn't arrest me for DUI or for Actual Physical Control of a Motor Vehicle. He could charge me with public intoxication if he were dickish enough about it, but I'd talked my way out of that on more than one occasion.

The cop car came to a halt in the dirt, and the driver door opened, those blue and red flashing lights still revolving in my rearview. The space around our cars was shrouded in trees, only a thin clearing of dirt connecting our vehicles. The trail road behind him, the lake in front of me. Even if I'd had my car keys, I couldn't have gotten past him.

I blinked a few times, preparing myself for a field sobriety test, probably right here in the dirt next to my car. Rested my hands on the steering wheel at 10 and 2.

"Driver," a megaphone voice said, even though the cop had parked only a hundred feet behind me. "Stick your hands out of the side of your vehicle."

Strange. Never heard that one before. I leaned over, pointing both my hands out the open window of the Jeep. Crickets chirped as I waited for the next command.

"Reach out and open the car door with your left hand."

The paranoia in his tone of voice made no sense. I was just sitting here by the water, not doing much of anything, but this cop was treating me like an armed suspect. I had no guns or weapons in the car, just the bourbon and a few painkillers stashed under the floor mats.

But I knew better than to bare my chest at the law, so I did as he commanded. Then I put one foot on the ground as the hammer of his revolver cocked back.

"Officer," I said, freezing in place. "Please don't shoot. I'm unarmed and I'm fully cooperating."

I didn't turn toward him, but I could now hear the clink of the handcuffs on his belt rattle as he jogged toward my car.

"Did I tell you to speak?" he said, almost growling.

I pressed my lips together and kept my hands out. The guy was having a bad day, and I had no choice but to ride it out. Clearly, this was the kind of insecure cop who'd arrest me for looking at him funny. Stillwater seemed to be infested with them.

He stopped five feet from me. The headlights from his car lit up his black boots, and I lifted my eyes to meet his. Short guy, stocky, tan uniform, wearing a cowboy hat with aviators perched on top. Gun in one hand, bulky flashlight in the other.

For a second, I thought he might not be real police, but then I noticed the badge hanging from his belt loop. And the very real gun in his hand.

"Get out of the car, slowly. If you do anything I don't like, I ain't going to hesitate to shoot. You read me?"

I nodded and dropped my other foot on the ground. Had a momentary flash of panic that this cop somehow knew who I was. Knew about my association with the Sinaloa cartel. That would explain his heightened paranoia and aggressive tone.

With both feet on the ground, I raised my hands and slid my butt off the car seat. Stood, frozen, next to my Jeep. I tried not to look him in the eye as he took another step closer to me.

He lowered the pistol. "What's your name, son?"

"Francis," I said. "Francis Walthrop."

He holstered his pistol and swished his lips around, thinking. "Francis, huh?"

"Yessir."

"You look a little old to be in school here."

"I'm twenty-six. I'm a grad student and a T.A. for the Agricultural Department."

"Uh-huh. You been drinking tonight, Francis?"

"No, sir."

He raised the flashlight, resting the hilt on his shoulder and keeping his grip on the base. Like a baseball bat, he could swing that thing at my head faster than I'd be able to dodge.

He pointed the blinding beam directly at my eyes, and I winced in response.

"Bullshit. I can smell it on you from here."

I shrugged. "I'm not causing any trouble, officer. Just came out here to think."

"Think?" he said, his face pulling into a sneer.

"Yeah. I'm not driving anywhere tonight, so maybe you can let me slide this time?"

A look of incredulity seized his face. He stomped across the dirt and froze six inches from me. He bared his teeth, and I could smell roast beef on his breath.

"Let you slide? Maybe you don't know it, son, but this lake has a curfew."

"I wasn't aware, officer. I didn't mean any harm."

"So, you're too stupid to look up the rules and regs of Payne County. Ignorance of the law is a shit excuse."

I gritted my teeth. Knew I had to play the power trip game, but it was getting harder and harder. "Like I said, I'm not causing any trouble. I did have a couple drinks out here, so if you'd let me get my phone out of the glove box, I can call a friend and have someone come get me."

He twisted the hand that clutched the base of the flashlight, like a batter testing his grip. I felt myself leaning away from him. He wanted to hit me. I could tell.

"I don't like your tone, boy."

"What tone is that?"

As soon as I'd said it, I knew it was a mistake. But it was too late.

He swung the flashlight at my head, and I couldn't dodge quickly enough. But as drunk as I was, I did manage to avoid the brunt. The hilt barely grazed my cheek.

He swung again, this time at my arm, and a blast of pain raced from my bicep up through my shoulder. A shock like fireworks blossomed and mixed with the adrenaline.

With no time to think, I reacted. I shot out my right and cracked him in the jaw. I followed with a left to his gut, but I was too slow. Felt sloshy and the world didn't move as fast as I wanted.

He pulled away from me, and one of his hands reached toward the pistol on his belt. He wasn't going to arrest me. He was going to shoot me. I had no doubt in my mind this guy was a power-tripping psycho.

Maybe coming out to the lake to beat up college kids was how this officer of the law got his kicks. I hadn't played along, so now I'd be punished.

I jabbed my fingers at his neck and felt them connect with his Adam's apple. He stumbled back a step, stunned. His hands flew to where I'd struck him, and he opened his mouth, struggling to breathe.

Escape. Now.

I pivoted, trying to race past him, but he jabbed out a foot and tripped me. I tasted dirt as I landed on my face. Before I could push myself to my feet, a massive weight fell on top of me and he flipped me over.

His hands wrapped around my throat. His fingers dug into my flesh.

"Enough!" he said, spittle flying from his lips. "I've had enough of you little shits!"

As his grip tightened around my windpipe, an enormous pressure built inside my head. He was shouting, but I couldn't hear it anymore because the pulse thudding in my ears outweighed everything.

I started to feel woozy. Was going to pass out at any second. As the headlights of his car began to fade to blackness, I had one blurry thought: my hands were free.

Do something. Do it now or you're dead.

I reached up and plucked the .357 from his side holster, pointed it at his chest, and jerked the trigger.

The bullet passed from the gun into his body in an instant. Like flicking on a light switch. No resistance, no hesitation, only a squeeze of my finger, and then a blast to light up the night sky.

The boom of the gun brought me back to reality. A million white dots sprinkled my vision as he slumped onto me. Wetness on my chest. A large frame, bearing down on me. At first squirming and writhing, then he slowed as the life rushed out of him.

With a grunt, I scooted out from underneath him. Gasping, wheezing, trying to regain my breath.

He plopped into the dirt, arms and legs splayed out. His head was to the side, eyes open, darting back and forth.

The gun shook in my hand. The cop stayed on the ground, and a pool of blood had already started to spread out from the hole in his chest.

His lids blinked rapidly, and his mouth worked up and down, but no words came out. He looked up at me, confused, terrified. The color had already begun to drain from his cheeks. His eyes darted in every direction, then they froze as he stared blankly into the trees.

I shot a cop.

Shot him in the chest.

But he was going to kill me, wasn't he? I hadn't

imagined that. This was happening. This was really happening.

The gun slipped from my fingers. "Oh, fuck me."

My throat burned. The reality of the situation was beginning to settle on me, and I couldn't have that. This couldn't be real, and I had to make it go away.

I raced back over to my car, flipped up the floor mat, and snatched my little cache of Percocet. I dry swallowed a couple of the painkillers and slipped into a blackout within seconds.

CHAPTER FIVE

My eyes were closed, lids tightly pressed together. A cold wetness brushed against my legs. My head throbbed, my arm didn't work, and stingers of pain danced all over my neck.

When I angled my head from side to side, it was like pushing through some kind of gel. The air around me didn't want to let me pass.

Painkillers. I had a vague memory of downing some Percocets, but that was the last thing I could recall. Had I been at the Stonewall bar last night? Maybe stumbled onto some random campus keg party?

No, that couldn't be it. Not many keg parties in the summer.

I opened my eyes, and I wasn't in the bathtub of some fraternity house. I was at the lake, in daylight. The rising sun beat down on the rippled water, making it shine like glass. Lake Carl Blackwell. I was alone. I'd been here since last night. Bits and pieces were coming back, but why had I stayed here last night?

I was on the bank, feet in the water. My jeans were soaked up to my thighs, and I was shirtless. So weird.

I looked down at my arm, at an oblong bruise on my bicep. That could have come from any number of places. What time was it? I needed to check in with Pug and everyone back in OKC.

I reached down to pluck my phone from my pocket, but instead of a phone, my hand touched the hilt of a .357 revolver, jammed into my waistband.

I blinked and hoisted the gun in my hand. I'd never seen this gun before, so how the hell did it find its way into my waistband?

Wait. No, I had seen this gun before. I'd fired it. Fired it at a person who had been trying to hurt me.

And that's when I remembered everything.

I'd killed a cop last night because he'd been trying to choke me to death. I hadn't wanted to kill him, but there hadn't been any other choice. His life or mine.

I'd never killed anyone before. Sure, I'd been in fights. Put people in the hospital. They'd all been scumbags who deserved it, like the pedophile in Mannford yesterday.

But never this. Never taken a life.

"What did I do?"

The gentle swishing of the water at the bank of the lake was the only sound that came back.

I stood, feeling wobbly. Stumbled back to my car, eyes flicking around the seats to find anything familiar. Boba Fett was still resting on the dashboard. My fifth of Evan Williams, now drained to an inch of brown liquid, sat idly on the passenger seat. Last I remembered, it had been at least half full.

And then I realized that the cop's body wasn't anywhere to be found. I'd killed him a few feet from the car. Could see the dark stain of his blood in the dirt.

What happened to his body?

"Oh, no. No no no."

I dashed into the trees on either side of my car. Nothing. I raced back toward the lake trail road, where a blast of sunlight blinded me. I held up my hands to block it, looked down the trail toward Highway 51, and saw nothing. Turned back left to find the squad car parked a few hundred feet up.

So, the cop's car was still here. Not where I'd last seen it, but it was still at the lake.

After pausing to puke, I stumbled along the gravel trail road to the car and found it empty. No dead cop, no nothing. Just an empty car sitting by the side of this trail road, a sheen of morning dew like beer can condensation lining the exterior.

My t-shirt was sitting in the grass next to the car.

Okay, so I had moved the car at some point last

night. No other explanation. For some reason, I'd driven this car a few hundred feet away from the spot where I'd killed its owner.

If I'd moved the car, my prints would be everywhere.

I picked up my t-shirt, opened the car door, and wiped off the steering wheel, the center console, and anything else I could think of that I might have touched. Then I closed the door and polished the door handle.

My head sloshed with post-painkiller jelly, and my knees became weak. None of this made any sense.

What had I done with his body?

My legs wobbled, and I sat, involuntarily. Dry heaved in the dirt a couple times, then had to catch my breath. If I had bothered to move the cop's car down the trail, then I must have done something with his body. Unless someone else had discovered the body.

I checked my phone for any evidence of last night, but I'd deleted all of my recent texts and the call log for the last week. Why would I have done that?

"What the hell is going on here?"

I needed to leave, now.

When I could stand again, I lumbered down the road, trying to find the spot I'd hidden my keys. Spent five minutes looking for them until I realized they were in my pocket. I returned to my Jeep and heaved myself into the driver seat. Took a long look out at the lake, hoping to see a body floating out there. Nothing but calm water.

This situation was bad. But the longer I stayed, the more dangerous it became. That cop's car probably had GPS on it, and the search posse would be here at any second.

Unless they already knew, somehow. If they did, why wasn't I in cuffs right now?

I hated having so many questions and no answers.

I had to flee the country. That was the only possible avenue I had left. Maybe I could go to Ramón, explain the situation, and he would sneak me into Mexico. I could work for our people down there until I could find the means to escape and make a living some other way.

Maybe Ramón would be willing to do this one favor for me.

Yeah, right. Ramón would shoot me on the spot.

CHAPTER SIX

WHEN I AWOKE in my bed, darkness filtered in through the windows. My eyes adjusted, and relief washed over me when I realized I was in my apartment. In my bed. Not in Oklahoma City at the Freedom House, not in jail, not in a coffin underground.

Home.

I powered on my phone to check the time. 7 pm. Notifications of several voicemails and texts from Pug and others popped up, but I ignored them. Didn't want to listen to or read messages from anyone.

If I talked to people I knew, I might have to tell them what I'd done the night before, and I couldn't imagine those words coming out of my mouth. As long as it was a secret, I had some power over it. Had some control and I could shake it like a bad dream.

When I stood, my whole body ached. That cop had beat the crap out of me, although I could only recall flashes of the events. The evil on his face. The desire to kill me. His hands around my throat, spittle flying from his lips as he screamed at me.

Maybe he'd known who I was, or maybe he was just a power-tripping asshole who killed for fun or some twisted sense of justice. Didn't matter.

What had I done with his body? No matter what other pieces of the night returned, that part eluded me.

I crossed the room into my "kitchen" to grab a beer from the fridge. Tossed the bottle cap into the sink and then rounded the room's divider to slump into the Papasan chair that filled most of my living room. I didn't have a couch. No television. Just my comfy chair and a couple of stools and milk crates for when people came over.

I sipped the beer, trying to figure out what the hell I was going to do next. Fleeing the country was still the preferable option. But, since I'd lost my passport years before, I couldn't legally go to Mexico or Canada. Maybe I could apply for a replacement passport, but that might take weeks. Besides, no way was I going to walk into the county clerk's office only one day after killing a police officer.

I never wanted to speak to any law enforcement ever again.

So, making my exodus through legal routes was out

of the question. Asking Ramón for help to leave the country was probably also unrealistic. I could possibly go above Ramón's head and ask his boss Gustavo, but I had no reason to think he'd do me the favor of arranging a reverse-coyote for me.

I'd tried nothing, and I was all out of ideas.

When the beer was gone, I returned to the fridge for another, but my stock was empty. I didn't feel like drinking the watered-down, store-bought 3.2 beer, which meant a trip to the liquor store, which meant I would have to bring it home warm and wait an hour for it to chill in the freezer.

So, to the bar I went.

I settled on Willie's Saloon, a dingy wood-paneled country bar about a block from my house. I trundled down the wooden steps outside my apartment, across the gravel parking lot, and rounded the side of the plasma center to reach it.

Willie's wasn't anything special, but I was sorta friendly with one of the bartenders who slung drinks most nights.

I opened the heavy door to the scent of peanuts and beer. On a little stage off to the right, a trio of women played guitar and chirped some red dirt song about summer lightning storms in Guthrie. I used to play guitar, but had busted three of my Ovation's strings six months before, and hadn't gotten around to replacing them. Something higher on the priority list always crowded out taking time to go to the music store. I did miss it sometimes, though.

The bar was mostly empty, surprising for a Friday night. Maybe because it was between summer school sessions, or maybe because it was still early in the evening. Either way, I liked it better. Didn't enjoy having to bump elbows with a bunch of rowdy college kids or shit-kicking locals.

I sidled up to the bar and nodded at Krista, my favorite bartender. Red hair, green eyes, a slim and trim figure, she was that elusive white whale who wouldn't ever let me take her home. Flirty as hell, but always kept me at a distance. On weeknights, when the bar thinned out, she would have drinks with me and tell me stories about growing up in a little West Texas town. We'd stare into each other's eyes and then she'd eventually go cold. I never could figure out if I kept pursuing her because I wanted her, or because she wouldn't let me have her.

She stopped in front of me, cleaning a glass with a hand towel. "Hey, Mike, haven't seen you around in a couple days. Been out of town?"

"I sure have. You hear about that terrorist attack that was supposed to go down in Vienna?"

"Um, no," she said as she cocked her head and gave me half a smile.

I knowingly tapped the side of my nose. "Exactly."

"Off serving your country, were you?"

"I can't confirm or deny that," I said with a shrug.

"I'll always remember you for your bravery, Mike. Now what can I get this patriot to drink tonight?"

I grinned, suddenly struck by the feeling that Krista reminded me a lot of Pug. Same quick and deadly wit. "I'll take a Harp, please."

She popped the newly-clean glass under a tap and filled it with the foamy, golden-brown liquid. "I'm glad to see you made it out alive."

"Me too," I said as I wiped my sweaty palms on my shorts.

She flicked her head at me. "What happened to your cheek? Fighting off an insurgent?"

What had happened was that a psycho cop had smacked me with his flashlight and then tried to strangle me, but Krista and I weren't close enough to share those details. She had no clue that I broke drug dealers' thumbs for a living. "Got into it with a Sigma Chi asshole last night. He thought I dented his bumper."

She grinned and placed the beer in front of me. "Did you?"

"I would never do such a thing, Krista. You know me better than that."

"Uh-huh," she said as she gazed down the other way along the bar. Some redneck in a flannel shirt trying to get her attention, poking an urgent finger at his empty glass.

Since I was starting to lose her, I reached across the bar and touched her forearm. "Wait, please."

She raised her eyebrows at me. "What's up?"

"What are you doing after you get off tonight?"

"I have to be up early in the morning."

"Will you stay after close and have one drink with me?"

She frowned, a pitying look. "Sorry, Mike. Some other time."

"Some other time," I said, and tilted back the glass. She waited a moment more with me—probably just being kind—then she eased back down the bar to help the insistent redneck.

Some other time.

Three hours later, I'd slugged enough Harp and Crown Royal shots to almost forget that I'd killed a person twenty-four hours before. I say *almost* because I didn't know if there was enough booze in the state of Oklahoma to wash away the grimy feeling of dread that seemed to cling to my skin like a wet t-shirt.

If I couldn't forget, then at least I could get drunk enough that I wouldn't care anymore. So that's exactly what I did.

I also tried to prevent myself from thinking about ways that I might leave the country, because that seemed to be a dead end. Maybe an answer would magically appear before me.

Krista played all that *come-here-go-away* stuff she usually did with me, tossing winks while she helped other customers at the far end of the bar. I'm not sure what I expected from her, anyway. I wanted to sleep with her, sure, but I liked her more than that. And I didn't see any way I could make her my girlfriend. I had no illusions about being boyfriend material. I could list all the reasons why, not the least of which was that I worked for serious drug dealers who tended to frown on personal attachments.

When I stumbled out of Willie's at around midnight, I had an empty wallet and a head full of mush. My limbs worked, but not in the way I wanted them to. I only had a block to go to stumble back home, though.

Once my eyes adjusted to the streetlights on Washington, I changed my mind. Couldn't remember if Hideaway Pizza was open this late, but the desire for some hand-tossed pizza throttled my brain, and I could think of nothing else. As if on cue, my stomach grumbled, twisting itself into knots.

I plodded up Washington toward campus. The streets were slick with recent rain, gutters full of silty mud. The way the cars had been parked at an angle along the street felt like they were pointing at me. *There he is, look at him. Murderer, drug cartel soldier, a hopeless drunk. Not boyfriend material.*

Those things were true, of course. If I needed a

reminder, all I had to do was think about the last time I'd seen my brother and sister, three years ago. The looks on their faces when I tumbled down the stairs at my parents' house, and my parents then ordered me to leave. I hadn't been *trying* to ruin Christmas. It's not as if I deliberately set out to get too drunk to navigate basic stair-climbing.

I turned on University and then took a shortcut through the alley behind Hideaway, found myself having to squint to make out the halos around a group of people. Two guys, standing next to a dumpster, talking with a young woman. They were white, and she was black, and they weren't just *talking* to her. One was in front, and the other was behind, and she was attempting to walk away, but they wouldn't let her.

It's my policy not to get involved in these shenanigans. Given my profession, I do my best to keep a low profile in public. But, some kind of mixture of the Harp and the Crown Royal and the awful day I'd had made me pay attention.

Then one of the guys grabbed her by the wrist, and my internal trigger clicked. I have no idea why it happened, but I felt an irresistible urge to pound in the faces of these two assholes.

I stormed across the street. "Hey."

All three of them looked at me. At this hour, in this skinny back alley, we were alone out here. Nothing but a street dim from faraway lamp lights, the backs of buildings, and the tomcats among us.

"What do you want?" said the guy standing in front of her. He was wearing a do-rag on his head, like some kind of gangster. Probably a private school misfit, more likely. The one behind her slipped a hand in his pocket. Instinct told me to eliminate him first, in case he had brass knuckles or a roll of quarters. I'd pin his arms and then take him to the ground.

But no, that was silly. These were just privileged college idiots acting like assholes. They wouldn't be armed.

I looked directly at the young woman. "Are you okay?"

She frowned and looked at the do-rag guy, then pursed her lips. "I just want to go home."

I flexed my fists and balled them, but held them at waist-level. They both noticed it, however. Do-Rag narrowed his eyes and then sized me up. Kicking both of their asses was going to be fun.

The guy standing behind her cleared his throat. "Why don't you mind your own—"

I punched him in the face before he could finish the sentence. Felt his nose crunch underneath the force of my hand. The second time in two days that I'd broken someone's nose.

He lurched back as his hands rushed to his face.

Blood immediately dribbled from between his fingers. He stumbled back a step, bumping into the dumpster.

Do-Rag let go of the girl's wrist.

"Go," I shouted at her, and she didn't waste any time thinking about it. She tore off down the alley, and her footfalls disappeared around the edge of the building in two seconds.

Do-Rag guy swung at me, and I pulled back, a little too far. Drunker than I'd realized, I lost my balance and landed flat on my ass in the street.

He leaped for me, and I managed to spin out of the way before he'd toppled on me. He skidded on the slick street, and I punched him in the ear before he could get his bearings. The other guy was still hovering by the dumpster, staring at the blood on his hands.

I scrambled to rise to my feet so I could continue teaching him the lesson about being grabby with women. That's when, again for the second time in two days, the blue and red lights of a cop car bounced off the exteriors of the surfaces around me.

CHAPTER SEVEN

THE CONCRETE BENCH under my ass pressed on me like a blunted knife. At first, it had been fine. But you can only shift around so much when your ankles are chained.

The interior of the Stillwater Police Department didn't surprise me at all. Simple walls, windowed doors with crisscrossed safety glass. Benches lining the walls. On those benches, metal rings on top at intervals and rings below. They'd chained my ankles, but not my hands. Handcuffs dangled from the top metal rings.

I'd been sitting on this bench for hours. Maybe five, maybe six, but long enough that I'd sobered up. A couple hours ago, I'd gotten so bored I'd started playing with the handcuffs until a surly cop with a handlebar mustache stomped into the room and shouted at me to leave them alone, or he'd restrain my hands too. I was a good boy after that.

Despite the boredom, I couldn't sleep. Every time I closed my eyes, I felt that cop's fingers wrap around my throat. Felt myself squeezing the trigger of his gun. Felt his meaty frame slump on top of me.

What the hell had I done with his body?

Occasionally, a door on one end of the room would open, and a cop would escort someone in an orange jumpsuit from one end to the other. Aside from Handlebar Mustache cop's threats and having my fingerprints taken a few hours before that, the passersby were the only excitement in the room. I could hear a ticking clock somewhere, but I couldn't see it.

No one had told me what I'd been arrested for. I figured public intoxication was the most likely charge, maybe aggravated assault, if one of those frat boys decided to press charges. Or, maybe they knew about the cop at the lake and had been looking for me.

Either way, once Ramón and the others found out I'd been arrested, they'd probably kill me. Too much of a liability. I'd never seen anyone in the organization come back from jail. Never heard about anyone getting arrested, even. Those people were probably dealt with quietly.

And then, that far door opened again, and a gaunt cop stepped through it, cradling a clipboard under his armpit. He glanced at the clipboard, then up at me, and dug out a keyring lined with dozens of keys. He crossed the room and knelt in front of me.

"Mr. McBriar, I'm going to uncuff you now. You're going to stand up, and I'm going to escort you into Interrogation 1. If you try to run, I'm going to put you on the ground. If you do anything aggressive or anything else I don't like, I'm going to put you on the ground. That's a promise."

"Okay."

"Okay," he said, and then removed the shackles around my ankles.

I tried to stand, but was too wobbly, and he had to catch me. I desperately needed to get some food in me. Maybe in the interrogation room, I could sell my soul for a Coke and a bag of Doritos.

The cop's fingers dug into my forearm as he shoved me toward the near door.

"Easy," I said. "I'm cooperating."

"No talking."

He swiped a keycard to open that door, and he pushed me into a hallway. Laminated posters about workplace safety and employee assistance programs lined the walls. We stopped at the first door on the right, and he ushered me into a small room. Table with another one of those welded metal rings, two chairs, video camera mounted near the ceiling.

He pointed at a chair. "Sit. Wait here."

"You're not going to cuff me to it?"

He sneered. "You giving me lip, son?"

I shook my head and took my seat, not wanting to say anything. These guys could be so damn touchy. At this point, I was too tired to be a smart-ass, and I only wanted the whole thing over with. Take me to jail or whatever, just let me have some food and a horizontal surface where I can sleep.

He maintained his eyes on me as he backed out of the room and shut the door. It clicked behind me.

I waved to the camera, at whoever was on the other side of it. Wished I had Boba Fett with me, but he was in a plastic box somewhere, along with my keys and my wallet and phone. Boba would give me a pep talk. Make me feel like there were ways out of this situation aside from death or prison.

This room did have a visible clock on the wall. It was already past seven. Took me a second to realize that was seven in the *morning*. Maybe I had slept a little out there because it didn't seem possible that I could have been dormant on that bench for so long.

I watched that clock tick for two full hours before anything happened. Then, at 9:08, the door behind me opened. I watched a diminutive white woman with short, curly black hair and deeply tanned skin enter the room. Pants suit and a badge with a large V clipped to her chest.

In her hand, she was carrying a large folder.

She didn't introduce herself, but she walked around

the table and had a seat. Without looking at me, she removed a set of grainy black and white pictures from the folder and began placing them in front of me, one by one.

A picture of Ramón and me in mid-stride, crossing the street somewhere. I didn't recognize the background buildings.

A picture of me in my Jeep, driving Ramón's boss Gustavo, stopped at a traffic light. Didn't recognize the intersection.

A picture of me walking out of a house, with a gun in one hand and a gym bag in the other. That time, I remembered. I'd picked up a package of some expensive weed for Ramón in Dallas. Couldn't recall why I'd had my gun out.

Another picture of Ramón and me, this time standing behind the Freedom House. He was holding out a shotgun as I was reaching to take it from him.

She positioned five or six more pictures like this in two rows, facing me. The woman cleared her throat. "You been waiting long?"

I shrugged.

"I had to come down here from Tulsa. Got me out of bed, actually. I'm supposed to be on a plane to Washington this afternoon, but that seems off the table."

She didn't seem happy about this, and I almost asked if I was supposed to feel bad about that, but I advised myself to keep my mouth shut. Only idiots poked the bear.

"You getting arrested was not part of the plan," she said. "You've gone and messed up our timeline. I doubt that would trouble you, however."

I licked my lips and stared at her. She spoke in vague terms because she wanted me to ask questions. To get me talking and admit something. I knew that much.

"My name is Special Agent Delfino, and I work out of the field office in Tulsa. You have no idea who I am, but I've known who you are for quite some time now, Michael. I know all about you and your boss Ramón Frederico and his boss Gustavo Salazar. And I don't care about you, or even them, really. I'm interested in Gustavo's boss El Lobo. Also known as Luis Velasquez."

I couldn't help it. My eyebrows climbed at the mention of El Lobo's name.

Delfino smirked. "You know the name."

I shrugged again. He was the big cheese, the highest-ranking person in the cartel I'd ever been allowed to know about. The person responsible for Texas, Oklahoma, and Kansas. Gus talked to him, but to the rest of us, he might as well have been a mermaid or a unicorn or something else out of legend.

I'd never actually met the man, but I had laid eyes on him once when he'd come to Oklahoma City to meet with Gus. They hadn't let a little soldier like me anywhere near the big boss, of course. But we'd all been made aware that he was coming. Ramón had forced me to clean the toilet in his bathroom that day.

Delfino slid a sheet of paper from the envelope and traced a finger down some text. "They want to charge you with public intoxication and inciting a riot."

"Inciting a *what*?"

"Ahh, it speaks."

I slumped and clenched my jaw. She'd won that round. But, at least, that told me they didn't know about the cop at the lake. She would definitely have led with that.

That itch in my chest to take a drink started to climb. If I got out of here, I'd need to stop at the liquor store, first thing.

"But the problem, Michael, is that if I let them arrest you, we miss out on a big opportunity. Your public defender will get them to drop the Inciting charge, and you'll do ninety days in County for the PI. I'm sure you can do such a tiny stretch standing on your head. But, when you get out, Ramón Frederico will probably kill you, won't he? No way will he trust you again after you disappear for three months."

I didn't feel the need to inform her that I'd already come to that same conclusion. I tried to keep my face neutral, but I could tell she was reading everything in my eyes. This was my first experience with feds, but she was exactly like all the other cops. She sat there all smug, acting like she already knew everything.

Delfino leaned back and folded her arms, staring at me. This went on for ninety seconds. I knew because I counted the ticks of the clock as our eyes locked like we were both frozen in ice. She barely blinked during the stalemate.

Finally, I couldn't take the silence anymore. "What do you suggest?"

"I don't care about this," she said, pointing at the sheets of paper. "We could arrest you for much worse, but that's not what I want. I care about what you've seen on the inside. I care about El Lobo."

"I've never met him. He's too important."

"You're a resourceful guy, Mike. If you can give us something useful, we can work out a deal."

"What kind of deal?"

She pursed her lips. I had to assume she would try to be vague about this too. "That all depends."

"Screw that. I want immunity."

Delfino grinned again, and I was really starting to despise the smarmy look on her face. She glowered at me like I was trash and she made no effort to hide it.

"Immunity is at the federal prosecutors' discretion," she said. "I can tell you this, though: cooperate, and it goes better for you. Don't cooperate, and if you live long enough, you'll go down with the rest of them."

I shook my head and tapped my finger on the table. "Not good enough. No jail time. I want Witness Protection. I want to get the hell out of Oklahoma, and the government is going to pay for it. I want all of this in writing, or I walk. I don't give a shit what you charge me with."

She seemed genuinely surprised that I'd stood up for myself. Maybe she thought spending all night in jail might have dulled my willpower to nothingness, but this woman didn't know me at all.

She chewed on her lip for a few seconds and then let a prolonged sigh escape through her nose. "I'm going to ask them to release you, Michael, because every minute you're in jail makes it look increasingly suspicious to your cartel buddies. But don't you think for a second that you're free. I'll be working out of the field office here in town for the next couple weeks. We'll be in touch soon, and until then, you need to figure out what you'll contribute, if you want to save your ass."

CHAPTER EIGHT

I WAITED UNTIL I'd entered Oklahoma City and had parked in the lot at the Freedom House before I allowed myself a sip of the Wild Turkey I'd bought back in Stillwater. After a night in jail, I needed to get back here as soon as possible, and as I said before, I don't drive drunk.

In the parking lot, I glanced in all directions. Were there cameras perched on the duplexes across the street? Was the government watching this place with drones or a spy satellite?

They knew everything. Delfino had outlined the names of all the key players in the Oklahoma branch of the organization and the crimes they'd committed, including my own. Even about the tweaker I'd beaten up in Mannford two days ago.

She knew everything about me, too. My parents, my

brother and sister, where I'd grown up, how I'd joined the Sinaloa three years before, at Pug's suggestion.

Hearing his name out of her mouth was the most painful part. How could I let Pug go down with the rest of them? Seems I had no control over what would happen to him, and that powerlessness burned at me.

I checked the time on my phone, the first time I'd touched it since reclaiming my possessions from the Stillwater Police Department. Noon. When Ramón had kicked Pug and me out of his apartment, he hadn't said when to be back. But two whole days without checking in with the boss was something that might raise eyebrows.

As I sipped the whiskey, I conjured up my excuse. A girl, a keg party, and a bottle of Valium. That was good enough. He wouldn't be happy that I'd been absent, but he would believe the lie, at least. He'd rant and rave and talk about how I was *this close* to being excommunicated from the business.

With my phone out, I decided to finally check the messages Pug had left me from yesterday.

First message: "Mikey, it's me. We need to talk about what happened at the lake last night."

My heart thumped. So, I'd called Pug to come help me. It seemed so obvious now, but I'd been too frantic to consider it before.

Second message: "Where the hell are you? It's all taken care of, but we need to talk, pronto. Ramón needs us for a thing in a couple days. I covered for you, but he wasn't happy that you weren't here."

Shit.

The third message was more of the same. I stowed the Wild Turkey, chomped on a breath mint, and left the car. Prepared to go upstairs and take my punishment from Ramón.

Inside the Freedom House, the halfway house manager was sitting at his desk in his office. He glanced up at me with a guilty look on his face as I passed by. Quickly, he averted his eyes and kept his head down. I'd always wanted to walk into his office and ask him if he knew what went on upstairs. If he was being paid off, or if his family had been threatened so he would turn a blind eye.

Or maybe he was a plant from Special Agent Delfino. Recording everything we said and did. And if he was, did it matter? If Ramón and Gus found him out, they would string him up by his thumbs and slash a thousand cuts across his body.

They would do the same thing to me, too, if I agreed to help the feds. Life in jail or death by torture were not easy alternatives to face.

I labored up the stairs, my body still feeling wrecked by the beating the psycho cop had given me. I needed to sleep for two or three solid days and clear my head of all the nonsense. That wasn't likely to happen.

On the fourth floor, I stopped outside Ramón's

apartment and collected my thoughts. Took a deep breath and rounded the open door to find Ramón wearing a t-shirt and sweats, sitting on his couch. Hunched over his glass coffee table. A rolled-up hundred dollar bill sticking out of his nose, six slug-shaped lines of white powder in front of him. His eyes flicked at me, then he held up a finger. He snorted two of the lines through one nostril and then two more through the other, and he growled as he tilted his head back. Next to the lines sat a glass of water, and he dipped his fingers in the glass and then snorted the water from the crook of his knuckles.

He pointed at the floor across from the coffee table. I walked to my assigned spot.

"Where the hell have you been?" he said.

"You told me you didn't want to see me for a couple days."

He cocked his head and wrinkled his brow at me. "You trying to twist my words around?"

I bit my lip. Didn't know who could be more touchy: Ramón, or those cops back at the Stillwater PD.

"No, Ramón. I'm sorry. I must have misunderstood."

Ramón dropped the rolled-up hundred on the coffee table and stood, then he sauntered around the table to me. Stopped a few inches away, his belly brushing up against my arm. He reached into his pocket and removed a folding knife, which he proceeded to use to pick at his dirty fingernails.

"Right," he said. "Don't ever misunderstand me again."

Pug's fist sailed toward me, and I wasn't quick enough to swerve my head away to dodge. His gloved hand connected with my jaw, making my teeth clench involuntarily. I wiggled my face back and forth to clear the aftershock. I hoped everyone else in the gym wasn't watching the ass-whooping Pretty Boy Pug was giving me.

He grinned, his yellow mouth guard making his face look demonic. He bounced on the balls of his feet, circling his boxing gloves in the air like some kind of old-timey strongman.

He said something which I couldn't understand through that mouth guard.

I leaned back into the ropes and waved a hand in surrender. "Uncle," I said, panting. Getting into the ring with Pug when I was still buzzed from the Wild Turkey had not been the smartest idea.

He lifted a hand in acknowledgment and spit out his mouth guard. "Had enough?"

"Isn't it obvious?"

"Well, you *are* a glutton for punishment, so I wanted to give you a choice."

"Yeah, yeah, Pug. Would it kill you to let me win every once in a while?"

He swished his lips back and forth and studied the ceiling like he was considering it. "It might. But we'll never know, will we?"

"I suppose not."

He picked at the tape on his gloves and eyed me. "Ramón go easy on you?"

"Not really, but we're okay now. He mostly yelled and snorted endless amounts of coke. The guy's blood pressure has to be off the charts."

Pug shook his head. "I definitely prefer him when he's stoned. A lot less aggressive."

We exited the ring and sat on the rickety chairs next to it. The boxing gym was alive with sound and motion and the stink of sweat. Mostly, the stink of sweat. It was grimy and run down, but I loved this place. Dirt cheap to work out here, which I appreciated, and nobody cared who we were in a shit-hole like this. And Pug—for being a rather fancy and cultured gay man—seemed to love it too.

Pug helped me remove my gloves, then he leaned in close to whisper into my ear. "What the hell happened to you? Why did you disappear on me?"

For a moment, I considered telling him the truth. But Delfino's voice kept playing in my head, her warnings about not speaking a word of this to anyone. That any break in the secrecy would result in them charging me with every possible crime they could think of.

I promised myself I'd devise a way to keep Pug safe, but I couldn't say anything until I'd figured that out. With no ideas materializing yet, I'd had to assign that problem to the *later* bucket.

"After the lake, I needed a rest. To be invisible for a day or two so I could not think about anything."

"Understandable."

"Why didn't I leave with you?"

"You refused to go. Said you still needed time alone and wanted to be near the water."

Sounded like the kind of stupid thing I would have said. "I don't even remember what we did with the body, Pug."

He breathed, not answering at first. A guy carrying a foam pad crossed the space next to us, and Pug waited until he'd left our area. "If you don't remember, then you don't want to know. But no one will ever find him."

I couldn't look at Pug. Had to change the subject.

"How's the nest egg coming?"

He nodded. "Little by slowly. Still not where I want to be, but I checked in last week. Think I can get them to come down a little from the most recent asking price."

"That's good, right?"

"It is."

I hadn't ever understood why Pug was so hell-bent

on buying that stretch of barren land. "What in the world are you going to do with four hundred acres near a Podunk town like Maud?"

Pug raised his palms to the ceiling. "Doesn't matter. It's my birthright." He stood and slung his boxing gloves over his shoulder, then eyed me in a way that made me feel strangely guilty. "Late lunch?"

I didn't like the way he'd been staring at me, but maybe that was the paranoia eating at my stomach lining. In the last three days, I'd been assaulted by a cop, arrested, and threatened by both an FBI agent and my boss. Wasn't the most typical week for me.

CHAPTER NINE

THE NEXT MORNING, I relished the feeling of waking in my bed in Stillwater. Despite the hangover pounding behind my eyes, waking up here was still a mile better than cat-napping on a concrete bench in jail.

I'd dreamed about that feeling of the water lapping at my legs at the lake. The way that psycho cop's eyes bulged as he tried to squeeze the life out of me.

I turned over and noted an ashtray with a few joint roaches sitting on my nightstand. Had no memory of smoking pot last night, so it must have happened after finishing the bottle of Wild Turkey. I hardly ever smoked the devil's tobacco. Probably bummed the joints from my downstairs neighbor, because me trying to roll a joint was like watching a car crash in slow motion.

I hoped I hadn't said anything stupid to him.

Chances of me appearing debonair and swashbuckling after drinking a fifth of whiskey: slim to none.

Next to the ashtray sat Boba Fett, waiting for me to wake up.

"Morning, Boba."

Good morning, Michael, he said. *Sleep okay?*

"Not really. Don't feel like I slept at all. What happened last night?"

Don't ask me. You only took me out of your pocket before bed. I did see you texting someone or other before you hit the lights.

"Oh, shit." I snatched my phone from the floor and checked my messages. I'd sent a couple to Krista, asking her to come up to my apartment after her shift. Fortunately, she hadn't responded. I really needed to look into getting one of those apps that prevents you from drunk dialing or texting people. For an introvert, I seemed to have no trouble wanting to associate with people when I was hammered beyond repair.

A knock came at my door. When I sat up, the full weight of my hangover settled on me, and an urge to puke rumbled from my belly up into my throat. But it settled quickly, and I rose to my feet, stumbled to the door, and opened it before I realized I was wearing only my boxers.

On the walkway outside my apartment door stood Special Agent Delfino, wearing something meant to approximate civilian clothes. Jeans, t-shirt, Oklahoma State Cowboys baseball cap, sunglasses. Flat smile.

I glanced at her Cowboys hat. When I opened my mouth to speak, my jaw creaked. "Go Pokes, huh?"

"Morning, Michael," Delfino said. "When in Rome. Now, can I come in?"

"What if I say no?"

"That would be a bad choice. Not a smart idea for anyone to spot us out here, chatting like this. We're trying to keep this a quiet affair, or have you forgotten?"

I stood to the side, and she entered my apartment. Cast glances all around after she took off her sunglasses. The state of the McBriar apartment was especially messy today. Seemed I'd been rifling through my things last night, looking for something.

"I decorated myself, in case you were wondering."

"I can see that."

I slumped into my Papasan chair, and she frowned at the collection of stools and boxes that made up my other seating choices. She slid onto a milk crate.

"Beer?" I said.

"I need you to take this seriously. Your arrest changed things, but there's new information, so we were going to have to move up the timeline anyway."

My hangover swelled and rumbled behind my eyes like a hyperactive fish in a little bowl, sloshing the water while doing laps. Even so, my stomach rumbled.

Wondered if QuikTrip would still have any of those sausage breakfast burritos left.

"What new information?"

"Sources in Mexico have informed us that El Lobo is coming to Oklahoma for a visit, six days from now."

I shrugged. "So?"

"We're going to mic you and put you in a room with him."

I chuckled a little. "Yeah, right."

"I'm not joking. This is what has to happen."

"How exactly are you going to do that? Like I said, I've never met the guy. He's an important person. I'm just a foot soldier. Not even that. Mostly, I pick up packages, drop them off. Sometimes I deliver messages to people. I'm a glorified errand boy."

"But you always carry a gun," she said.

"Sometimes errands are dangerous."

"Cut the shit. We're not going to dwell in this small-timer fantasy. You're in the organization, and that makes you valuable."

If Delfino only knew how little value I held for them. "Why do you need this, anyway?"

"There's barely any real evidence that he even exists. It will help our case if we have tape of the two of you."

"Why?"

She sighed, exasperated. "It gives credence to your testimony if we can prove you've met him. Make it harder for the defense to poke holes when we can connect you all the way up the chain."

"There's no way you're going to get me into a room with Velasquez. It's not realistic."

"Maybe I should clarify. *You're* going to find a way to get yourself in a room with him. You're going to be mic'ed up, and you'll get him to talk about something at that meeting."

"What the hell would he want to talk to me about?"

"You figure that part out. Doesn't matter what. Doesn't even have to be something illegal. But you're going to engage with him. You can talk about baseball, for all I care."

"You have to be shitting me. Baseball?"

She cleared her throat. "That's how this is going to work. You do that, you agree to testify about all the other people you know, and you'll have your WitSec deal."

I glanced down at her empty hands. "Where's the paperwork?"

"It's only been a day, Michael. You'll have to give me some time. I'm working on it."

"Not just me."

"Excuse me?"

I sat up in the chair. "I want a new identity for Pug, too. His name is Phillip Gillespie, and he either comes with me, or I'm not doing jack shit."

Delfino shifted on the milk crate and shook her head. "That's outside our scope."

Anxiety gripped my chest, but I decided to press it anyway. "Figure it out. We're a package deal."

Her jaw clenched, and she stabbed a finger at me. "You think you have leverage here? You are dead wrong. And let me tell you this: if you warn your friend or do anything to put this operation in jeopardy, I'll make sure they file the maximum charges against both of you."

PART II

A SEAT AT THE TABLE

CHAPTER TEN

ONCE AGAIN, PUG and I found ourselves on the way to a drug dealer's house to deliver a message. Except this time, I was driving because Pug had smashed his hand in a door this morning, and he couldn't grip so well. Which meant no alcohol for me until the trip was done.

Also, we weren't visiting one of the dealers who worked for us. We were going to talk to a representative from a neighboring organization to ask them politely to stop moving crack cocaine into Oklahoma City. Was attracting too much bad attention from cops. Weed, prescription drugs, a little cocaine... they could mostly turn a blind eye. But heroin or crack? That was not a good idea. The Sinaloa was smart enough to know this. This other organization was not.

And finally, the main difference was that none of the

last trips Pug and I had taken together had come hours after I'd sat down in my living room with an FBI agent. I had a deal on the table, the chance to get out of here and start fresh. But I couldn't tell anyone about it, and I only had six days to find a way to earn an audience with El Lobo himself, Luis Velasquez. To get a seat at the table.

Such a thing was impossible. I tried not to think about it because I couldn't handle the fact that the whole thing was an exercise in futility.

"Hot as a stripper's butt crack today," Pug said.

For a second, the comment didn't register. I mumbled something that sounded like I agreed with him.

He pivoted in his seat, holding that swollen hand in the air. "What is wrong with you, Mike? You're all out of whack today. Yesterday, too."

I pointed to the still-visible bruises on my throat, the ones placed there by the psycho cop. Mentioning that seemed to be choosing the lesser of two evils.

"Right," he said, "that. I've been trying not to think about it, to be honest with you."

"Me too."

I studied Pug out of the corner of my eye. Did he believe me that the events had gone down the way I'd said they had? I had truthfully killed the cop in self-defense, but I debated if Pug would have still helped me hide the body if the cop's death hadn't been self-defense.

If I'd shot him to keep myself out of trouble or something like that.

Yeah, I think Pug would have helped me regardless. He was like that.

As we approached Tulsa on I-44, that whiff of familiarity warmed me. I'd grown up in this area, not far out of town. Something about that sense of seeing the same billboards and traveling on the same highways gave me comfort. I'd always assumed that I would eventually get someone pregnant, and then I'd be forced to settle down, pick a neighborhood for a school district, and get a real job. Either that or I'd die in a hail of bullets in the service of the cartel.

Or maybe neither. With this new FBI angle, my future was now entirely up in the air.

I pointed at a mass of black clouds to the east. "That looks not so good."

"Tornado season in Oklahoma," Pug said in his best redneck accent. "It's cheaper than a plane ticket, but might not get you exactly where you're trying to go."

Last year, a tornado had ripped an Oklahoma City suburb to shreds. One of those black funnels could spin down a street, toss one house into the air, but leave the next untouched. I had a lot of respect for the chaos and unpredictability of it. Five years ago, my New Jersey-native college roommate had freaked out when tornado sirens blasted across Stillwater one night. He started frantically searching Google Maps for a nearby house with a storm cellar. I laughed and told him we'd just take our beers out onto the porch. He thought I was crazy, but I said that if a twister was going to rip the house to pieces, there wasn't a thing we could do to stop it. Going into the basement wouldn't make any difference, so we might as well watch the show. The twister uprooted a few trees, then eventually veered away from Stillwater and returned to the sky without much fuss.

"What's that bar on Cherry Street you like?" Pug said.

"You mean Empire? Kilkenny's, maybe? All those places on that little strip are good. Hideaway Pizza, too."

A friend of mine once said that if you lived in Tulsa, were in your twenties, and weren't going to college, you needed to live on Cherry Street and work at the Hideaway. The idea had some romance to it as a Townie tradition. If this Witness Protection thing happened, I might never have Hideaway pizza again. Might never see this town and these familiar streets and billboards ever again, either.

Pug popped open the glove box and took out his pistol. He flexed his hand around the grip, grimacing. "I could definitely go for some pizza after this is over."

I eyed the gun. "You think we're going to need that? I mean, they're expecting us. Ramón told us this would be civil. Like a business meeting where we go over terms and come to an agreement."

"Come on, Mikey. Think about it. If they wanted to

have some sit-down love-fest, they wouldn't send us. Gustavo himself would have come if it was important."

"What are you saying? We're supposed to shoot up the place?"

Pug popped out the clip and checked the springiness of the bullets. "I think Ramón doesn't care one way or the other if we do. If it goes well, he gets what he wants. If we make trouble, he can distance himself from it all. And if we get shot up in the process, gives him an excuse to go to war."

I tapped the steering wheel a few times with the flat of my palm. Made perfect sense. "So what are we supposed to do?"

Pug flexed his injured hand again, wincing as he made a fist.

"We do our jobs, I guess."

East of Tulsa sat a little town named Sand Springs. Less of a town, really, and more like a meth cook audition factory. You'd run out of fingers and toes counting the blown-up houses as soon as you left the highway and ventured into the neighborhoods.

We knew the general area of the house we were looking for, but not the address. We found a trailer park on the edge of some woods, with the individual trailers at haphazard locations like blocks strewn across someone's front lawn. Little gravel streets carved between the plots. I crawled the neighborhood streets, slowing anytime we saw something that looked promising.

"What about that one?" Pug said, pointing at a trailer with bright yellow siding.

"Maybe. Would have been helpful to have an address."

"Ramón didn't think it would matter. They move around, I guess. I didn't think there'd be so many that we'd have to hunt for it."

"Let's give this one a whirl," I said as I turned into the little gravel circle in front of it and killed the engine.

We strutted up the wooden steps, and Pug rapped on the front door. The trailer felt cold and uninviting, but I suppose you could say that about most of them. We weren't likely to spot a *Bless This Mess* doormat sitting out front.

A moment later, the door creaked open and in the visible space appeared the two unmistakeable holes marking the snout of a double-barreled shotgun. Pointed right at Pug.

"Pug," I said.

He'd already seen it. He stepped back and raised his hands. The door creaked open a bit further, and there stood a wizened lady wearing a robe that drooped off her frame like a sheet hanging in the wind. She holding the shotgun loosely, her finger caressing the trigger. When she opened her mouth, she displayed a set of gray and black teeth.

"I don't know you," she said.

"We're sorry to bother you," I said. She pivoted, pointing the shotgun at me.

"What do you want?"

"We're looking for someone," Pug said.

She sneered. "You've got yourselves the wrong house. Ain't nobody here worth looking for."

"Clearly," I said.

"And you must think you're funny," she said.

Pug cleared his throat. "We're trying to find a couple of guys who have a trailer around here. Youngish? One of them has piercings."

"I don't know," she said, "and I wouldn't tell y'all nothing if I did. This ain't the kind of community where you can just come calling and think you're going to find answers. Now get the hell off my porch."

Pug and I backed down the steps slowly, our hands in the air. The shotgun lady didn't withdraw into her trailer until we were back at my Jeep.

We slid into our seats and breathed a simultaneous sigh of relief.

"Jesus Christ," Pug said. "God bless America, right?"

I started the car and backed out of her driveway. "Meth-heads, my dear Pugsley. Always a joy."

We continued around the lot but didn't approach any more trailers on foot, not until we were sure. We found a couple that looked promising, but I wasn't willing to stop until I had a good reason.

Then, one trailer was a bit back from the road, with its windows shrouded in tinfoil. Something told me this was the place.

"There," I said.

"Works for me," Pug said. "But I'm not walking up there blind. Honk the horn."

I did, and we vacated the car to sit on the hood of my Jeep, waiting, staring at that double-wide. But neither of us made a move to stroll up to the trailer. If this situation were going to explode, I'd rather do it outside, sweating under this July sun, with my car keys in hand.

"I don't know if they're coming out," Pug said.

"Fine with me if we sit out here for a little while."

Then, the tinfoil over one of the windows peeled back, and a pair of eyes materialized in the darkness. A moment later, the front door opened, and two men stomped onto the trailer's rotting front porch. They were both rail-thin, with pale and acne-scarred cheeks. The only way to tell them apart was that one wore a septum piercing hanging from his nose like a prized bull. I would have to guess twins, but didn't know for sure. Ramón hadn't given us their info.

The non-pierced one lifted a hand to his forehead to block out the sun. "Y'all from OKC?"

I nodded, and they left the porch but didn't cross the yard yet.

"What brings you up from the city on a hot-ass day like this?"

"You know why we're here," Pug said. "You're supposed to be expecting us."

Pierced One flicked his head toward the side of the house. "Let's go out to the river. Ain't safe to talk here."

I shrugged as Pug and I slipped off the hood of the car, then followed Pierced and Non-Pierced around the side of the house. The backyard quickly descended a grassy hill, which eventually ran into a river. To the left, the river widened, and a large camelback bridge sat over the water. Big rusted metal thing, more red than gray. A spiderweb of beams suspended fifty feet above the rushing water.

Our two hosts said nothing to us, and as long as they were leading the way, I kept my eyes on their hands and the backs of their waistbands. I couldn't see any guns sticking out, or bulges, for that matter. But they were both wearing jeans, so they could easily have concealed ankle holsters.

I didn't like that we were on their turf. I didn't like that our bosses hadn't been honest about our purpose for coming here.

They chatted with each other as we all angled down the slope of grass and brush toward the bridge. Pug and I shared a look, and he winked at me. I knew exactly what he was saying: *don't worry about this. It's just a couple of local redneck crackheads who are going to try to act tough, but if we apply a little pressure, they'll cave.*

They reached the bridge and walked halfway across it, then both of them took up a spot near one side, under the metal beams. Pug and I positioned ourselves opposite them on the other side of the bridge, twenty feet away.

"So," Pierced One said, the stainless steel in his nose wiggling as he talked, "what can we do for you?"

"Our employers… you know who that is, right?" I said, raising my voice to compensate for the sound of the river.

Both of them nodded. They flaunted condescending smirks on their faces, and that irritated me.

"They sent us here to ask you to consider an alternate route for your distribution. We don't have any stake in the crack game—"

"Damn straight," Non-Pierced One said as he spat a jet of brown tobacco juice onto the bridge. "You don't got a stake, so you don't have any right telling us what is and ain't our business. What makes you think y'all can come up in here and start telling us how to run things?"

I took a breath, reminded myself to be calm. No one had to die out here today.

"I think maybe you have the wrong impression," Pug said. "We're only trying to talk about what's in our combined best interest. Attracting the wrong kind of attention hurts everyone."

Pierced One gritted his teeth. "You OKC people think you run the whole damn show, and we're just in your shadow."

"We're not trying to tell you how to run your business," I said. "Our employers sent us here—"

Like a flash, Pierced One whipped a gun out of an ankle holster. He didn't raise the gun, instead kept it pointed at the ground, but he did take a step forward.

I resisted the urge to whip out my Beretta. There had to be a way to fix this.

"Why you keep telling us about your employers?" Pierced One said. "Do you know who *we* work for? You think we're scared of you on account of the fact y'all work for some goddamn wetbacks with guns?"

Pug's hand drifted to the back of his jeans, near his pistol. I kept my hands at my sides.

"Maybe we could start this over," I said. "Seems like we haven't explained ourselves properly."

Before I could get out another word, Pierced One raised his gun and jerked the trigger. The bullet sailed just over my shoulder. I dropped to my knees and snatched the Beretta from the back of my waistband, ears already ringing from the blast. By the time I'd had it up and ready, Pug was barreling forward, aimed at Pierced One's knees.

I couldn't get the shot.

I pivoted, pointing the gun at Non-Pierced One,

who was struggling to free his gun from an ankle holster. He met my eyes, frantic.

"Don't move!" I said.

But he wouldn't listen. He hiked up his pants, wrapped his hand around the grip of a 9mm.

I pulled the trigger. The shot echoed along the frame of the bridge as the bullet tore a hole in his throat. He tumbled away from me, bending backward over the railing of the bridge, then he plummeted into the water. *Splash*.

Both Pug and Pierced One, who had been wrestling on the ground, stopped to watch his body drift along the river. Pug recovered first and snatched the gun from the guy's hands. They were bunched together, and I still couldn't find a clean shot that might not accidentally hit Pug.

As my friend scrambled to rise to his feet, Pierced One threw a shoulder into Pug's hip to knock him to the side.

Their bodies separated and I saw my chance. I lifted the pistol to shoot at Pierced One, but my fingers were sweaty. I couldn't find the trigger. Then, he jumped up and leaped over the edge of the bridge, disappearing into the river below.

Pug and I dashed to the other side. The rushing water sped the guy down the river, and Pug raised his gun and squeezed off one shot. Missed.

In another moment, he was far enough away that there was no point in wasting any more bullets.

I smacked the butt of my Beretta on the bridge. It clanged back at me. "Damn."

"Think we should wait for him back at the trailer?" Pug said.

I shook my head. "Doubt he's going home."

"Well, shit. I guess Ramón and Gus are going to get the war they wanted, anyway."

CHAPTER ELEVEN

PUG AND I hadn't talked much about what happened at the bridge on our way from Sand Springs to OKC. I kept imagining ways I could have handled it better, but each path ended the same way in my head. I could not envision a scenario that didn't end with those guys pulling their guns on us. Stupid rednecks. It wasn't a matter of our negotiation skills being subpar. Just what happens when you try to reason with cracked-out drug dealers in the boonies.

One thing, though, I knew for sure: Ramón would have heard about it by the time we'd returned. He had some superhuman screw-up detector. And I also knew that this time, I wasn't going to let him backhand Pug for no good reason. This was nobody's fault, and if Ramón decided otherwise, then to hell with him.

Close to the Freedom House, Pug got a text that we

were to report to the warehouse in Del City, a structure that had been part of Tinker Air Force Base at one time but was no longer in use. We sometimes used it as a covert distribution center for arranging high-volume shipments.

Since I didn't know of any major shipments we'd been coordinating, meeting at the warehouse couldn't be good news.

Del City seemed especially barren today, and the heat radiated off the streets like waves of burning air above the asphalt. As I parked at the warehouse parking lot, I turned to Pug and said, "we did everything we could."

"Won't matter. Even if this outcome is what Ramón wanted, he'll still find a way to freak out about it." He put his head in his hands and then dragged clawed fingers down his face, leaving trails of white that faded back to skin-color.

"I've had about enough of this," he said.

I gripped the steering wheel and kept my mouth shut. Couldn't reconcile how badly I wanted to inform Pug about Agent Delfino's deal with her fierce order that I not tell a soul. And then I felt guilty for keeping this secret from my best friend. Pug would never do that to me.

"It won't be like this forever," I said.

"That's the truth," Pug said as he abandoned the car and marched toward the warehouse door.

Inside, we found no boxes in preparation for shipping. Instead, I only saw a ring of people in the center of the enormous and empty room. Ramón, a few thugs from Freedom House I recognized, and one person in the middle of the ring, sitting in a chair with his arms and feet bound.

Ramón and some of the others turned and pointed guns at us as we walked in, then quickly lowered their weapons. Ramón waved us over. At Ramón's left stood Tanner, a baby-faced teenager. I knew his name because he stayed in the apartment next door to Ramón.

Tanner weighed and bagged, a task Ramón liked to assign to the youngest in the crew. They didn't have to learn how to handle guns, only scales and packaging techniques. He thought the young ones were less likely to steal, or at least easier to control.

I didn't know the name of the person tied to the chair in the center of the circle, but I did recognize him. I'd seen him around the Freedom House a couple times, but not for at least a year or two. This prisoner looked to be mid-twenties. His face was a bloody and bruised mess, and his retro Tulsa Roughnecks t-shirt was bloodied to a dim red. Someone had been working him over for at least an hour or two.

The guy standing to Ramón's right tightened the bloody rags wrapped around his knuckles. And Ramón was holding a black baton, about eighteen inches long.

"What's going on here?" Pug said as we joined the circle.

Ramón pointed his baton at the bloody man in the chair. "You remember Steven?"

I squinted at the man and repeated the name a few times to myself. I did remember him now. He had been one of Ramón's delivery drivers a few years back. One day, without warning, he'd disappeared, and hadn't ever been seen again. Until now.

But Pug and I both kept our mouths shut.

Ramón knelt and tapped the baton on the concrete floor of the warehouse. The echo sustained in the grand room. "Where did you go, Steven?"

Blood dribbled out of Steven's mouth when he spoke. "Idaho."

"Idaho," Ramón said, musing on the word. Then he pointed the baton at Tanner. "If Tanner hadn't seen you at the gas station, would we have known you were in town?"

Steven shook his head.

"Ahh," Ramón said. "That is unfortunate. Tell me, why did you come back?"

"My mother," Steven said. "She got sick."

"Your mother," Ramón said wistfully. This copycat game was starting to freak me out.

And then, Steven looked up and met my eyes. Maybe I'd imagined it, but for a second, I felt like he could see right into me. That he knew I'd been talking with federal agents and had been in the process of securing a WitSec deal. Had Steven tried the same thing, only to get caught coming back to visit his family?

"You didn't call, you didn't write," Ramón said. "You didn't tell us anything when you disappeared."

"I'm sorry."

"Is your mother feeling better?"

Steven shook his head, wincing. "No, she's dying."

Ramón rose to his feet and lifted the baton above his head. "Well then, Steven, I hope it was worth it."

I closed my eyes as Ramón swung the baton at Steven's knee.

CHAPTER TWELVE

I SAT ON my usual stool at Willie's Saloon, waiting for my favorite bartender Krista to make an appearance. No luck so far. Maybe she had the night off. I wasn't in any shape to be on my flirt game tonight, but maybe I needed someone to make me feel like I wasn't a steaming pile of dog shit. Attention from a pretty girl could have that effect on me.

Ramón hadn't said a word to us about Sand Springs and our task there. Maybe he'd been too distracted by dealing with prodigal son Steven to remember he'd manipulated us into starting a war on his behalf.

I kept pounding draft beers and whiskey chasers, trying to disable my brain, or at least mute it. Didn't work. I couldn't seem to get drunk, no matter how much I consumed. My belly was full and every time I got up to use the bathroom, I wobbled a bit, but my head felt as clear as a sunny day.

What plagued me the most was how much less it had bothered me to kill the crackhead this morning, compared to killing the cop three days ago. Either a crackhead's life was worth less to me, or killing had become easier. That proposition didn't seem easy to swallow. I never wanted killing to feel easy.

I never wanted to kill at all, as a matter of fact.

Every time I closed my eyes, I saw Ramón's baton crash into Steven's knee, the way it made a sound like an egg cracking. Then, whenever I opened my eyes, I visualized the bullet from my gun punching a hole in the throat of that crackhead in Sand Springs, and then him topple off the bridge railing into the river.

Since I couldn't erase my thoughts, I spent some time trying to connect the dots. A gang war with these Tulsa crackheads was imminent. Since Ramón himself hadn't mentioned anything about the deal not going well in Sand Springs, war had clearly been the true goal from the start.

If these crackheads murdered me, then I wouldn't have to worry about this whole Witness Protection thing. That was a plus. I did conjure up plenty of downsides, though. If this gang war escalated and other Sinaloa members died, the feds might call off the deal if they found no one left to arrest. Or, what if El Lobo himself ended up on the wrong end of a gun? Hard to imagine a scenario where I might have to protect the assholes I worked for so they could live long enough to be arrested.

So, El Lobo had to live. Problem number one. But, even if he survived this coming war (if it did happen), I still had to gain an audience with him. Not only that, I had to persuade him to chat with me, all while I'd be wired for sound. And I only had six days remaining to invent a way to do all that while keeping Pug safe.

Not a chance in hell.

In the far corner of the bar, two drinkers started arguing about politics. Something about what Congress had done, and I had no clue what they were talking about. I was so far from being involved in the outside world, bits and pieces of news I gleaned always sounded like fiction to me.

I fished Boba Fett's head out of my pocket and set him on the bar in front of me. "Crazy shit today."

Sure was, Boba said. *Your days have been more and more like this lately.*

"I killed someone else today. Shot this crackhead."

I know. I was there. You going to tell Pug about your visit from the feds?

"Delfino said my WitSec deal would be void if I did."

Doesn't mean you won't do it.

I sipped my beer. Couldn't taste it anymore. "True, but I've been thinking about that. I've got a plan. I'll go along with what they want and play the game. Then, when it comes time to testify, I'll leave Pug out of it. Claim he didn't do anything illegal at all. That way, I get what I want, and he doesn't face any jail time."

Sounds risky.

"Yeah, but I don't see any other way that doesn't end with Pug taking the rap with everyone else."

Maybe it works, or maybe they scrap your deal if you perjure yourself.

I wanted to argue with him, but I couldn't find a way. "Not looking good, is it?"

No, Michael, it's not. But you have to stick with it.

"I do? Why? What happens if I end up like that guy Steven, beaten mostly to death in a warehouse somewhere?"

You're smarter than that.

I noticed a couple people at the other end of the bar raise eyebrows at me, but I didn't pay too much attention. It's like they'd never seen a guy talking to a Star Wars action figure before.

"Am I smarter?" I said. "Not sure about that. I have no idea what I'm doing. I don't know why I should keep on trying to put this puzzle together."

Because failure is not an option. You don't come through on this WitSec deal, you're flushing your life down the drain.

I tilted back my amber glass of Harp, draining it to the foamy dregs. "Boba, my life is already over. It ended the day I first started working for these people."

I lifted the glass and jiggled it at the bartender until

I'd earned his attention, and he held up a finger to tell me to wait.

Hold on, Michael, Boba said. *You have to listen to me. There has to be more than this. There has to be a way out of all this.*

"Who knows?" I said as the bartender moseyed down to me and I pointed at my glass for a refill.

Was there more than this? A way out?

Maybe so, but I sure as hell had no idea what that way out would look like.

CHAPTER THIRTEEN

GUSTAVO SALAZAR, MY... grandboss, I suppose you could say, had a house in the northwest area of Oklahoma City. The nice part of town, with all the old oil money. I don't know what Gus wrote down for *occupation* on his taxes, but it had to be something clever. He had a gargantuan stone house set back from the road in the Nichols Hills neighborhood. With acres of tree-covered land surrounding it and a few other structures aside from the main residence, Gus's house was more like a compound than a home. Even more so because he was hardly ever there, but his security guards were always patrolling.

I waved at the security camera at the front gate, and after a thirty second pause, the iron bars creaked inward. I drove up to the house, hunting for other cars. Since Ramón was my boss, I shouldn't technically be here, doing what I was about to do. Seeking an audience privately with Gus. If Ramón found out, he would be furious. I didn't see his truck parked out front, which meant I was in the clear, for now.

I didn't know what I was going to say to Gus yet to persuade him to grant me close access to El Lobo. Gus had always seemed like a reasonable man to me, if not a little volatile. I mean, nothing like Ramón-level of psychosis, but Gus was quick to act if he thought someone was taking advantage of him.

I parked at the side of the circle drive and had a little sip from my flask. Not enough to affect me, but damn was my throat dry at that exact moment. I promised myself more once this was done, and that allowed me the ability to leave my flask behind without becoming too anxious about it. I covered up the smell with a big slug of my morning coffee, then also left that mug behind in the cupholder.

When I knocked at the door, no one came for ten or fifteen seconds. Finally, multiple locks unlatched from the inside, and the door opened no more than two inches. A familiar pair of eyes appeared in the crack.

"Is he expecting you?"

"Hey, Hank. Long time no see."

Hank didn't fall into my small-talk trap. "Is he expecting you?"

I shook my head. "It's important. I can wait if he's busy."

"What makes you think he's here today?"

I sighed. "Is he here today?"

Hank nodded and said nothing.

"Then can I come in and wait for him, Hank? Pretty-please?"

Hank breathed for a couple seconds, but he relented and opened the door for me. Hank was a beast of a man, at least 6'4", with orange tanning bed skin and muscles like a power lifter. The perma-scowl came naturally to him. Gus didn't usually hire smiley people to protect his home.

I stepped inside to a grand circular entryway with a twinkling chandelier above and a marble staircase snaking up to the second floor. I had to wonder how Ramón felt about living in that dingy apartment in the Freedom House while his boss lived in luxury twenty minutes away.

Hank adjusted the shoulder strap of his Heckler & Koch UMP submachine gun, then he pointed at a loveseat in the corner of the room. "He's in a meeting. Grab a seat."

"But you'll let him know I'm here, right?"

Hank frowned. "Sure, Mike. I'll let him know."

He left me there, his shoes clacking on the marble floor as he swept down a hallway. He tossed a glance before rounding the corner, his eyes following me until he'd disappeared. For some reason, Gustavo Salazar's entourage of security liked me less than Gus himself did. Don't ask me why.

I busied myself by playing some meaningless time-wasting game on my phone. One of those games where your character is moving endlessly, and you have to tap on the screen every few seconds to jump over obstacles in your path. No matter how many times you tap, you never get free of the obstacles. In this game, I was a skier in the Swiss Alps, cruising down a never-ending ski slope, jumping over rocks and trees trying to trip me.

A half hour passed, and I started to wonder if Hank had actually told Gus I was here. Wandering around to look for him probably wasn't a smart idea. I wasn't sure that some guard I didn't know might not shoot me first and ask my name after.

Also, the longer I waited, the greater the chance that Ramón might show up. If that happened, I wouldn't have a good explanation as to why I was going above his head. I couldn't even begin to think of an excuse that would sound believable.

On two different occasions, guards I'd never seen before strolled through the room, eying me as they did. Their looks reminded me of being in jail, chained to the bench. At least here, Gus' guards didn't bother to sneer at me like the cops had. No, these guys didn't have to make scary faces. They could shoot me without having to worry about filling out paperwork later.

Thirty more minutes dribbled by, and my phone battery dwindled as I grew tired of tapping on the screen to jump over rocks. The thought occurred to me to give up and try again later.

A throat cleared at the top of the stairs.

I looked up to see Gustavo Salazar standing there, leaning over the railing. Scar across his forehead like a deep wrinkle. The brown of his skin shone under the ample daylight in this grand entry room.

His head was cocked slightly to the left, a quizzical look on his sharp face.

"Michael? What are you doing here?" His voice echoed down the stairs to me.

"Can we talk?"

He frowned but waved me up to join him. I still wasn't sure what I would say, but chose to trust myself in the moment. Let the situation work itself out. I wasn't drunk, so I had most of my faculties about me.

As I crested the staircase, he slipped a business card from his back pocket and shuffled it into his crocodile skin wallet. I got a quick look at the raised image of a wolf's head on the card. El Lobo's calling card, the ones he gave out only to his captains and a few other top earners in the organization. Sort of a universal keycard for any Sinaloa-related gathering.

At one point early on, I'd entertained nihilistic fantasies about becoming a big player in the Sinaloa; becoming the kind of person who carried one of those cards. But it's not as if I ever had the chance to earn one. Plus, once I'd figured out how nefarious this whole organization could be, I didn't want one anymore.

"Thanks for seeing me, Mr. Salazar."

He returned the wallet to his back pocket and leaned against the railing of the stairs. "You can call me Gus, Michael. We are family."

"Thank you."

"What can I do for you?"

Moment of truth. "Well, it's just that... I heard some of the guys saying that Mr. Velasquez is coming into town in a few days."

He raised an eyebrow.

Oh, shit. Maybe when the feds had told me that, it was super top-secret. Maybe they'd overheard that information on a wiretap, and now Gus would know I'd gotten inside information somehow.

My head swam, and my palms became slick. I tried not to let my eyeballs bug out of my head.

Gus frowned. "Yes, it is true. But no one should be speaking of these things. When he moves from place to place, we must do everything we can to protect him, and that means keeping quiet. You haven't spoken this to anyone else, have you?"

"Of course not."

"Good." He lifted his palms to the air. "So, since you already know, what do you want to ask about his visit?"

I kept my exhalation of relief small, barely pushing

air out of my lungs. "I want to do more, Gus. I want a chance to impress El Lobo."

I didn't know if using Velasquez's nickname was a bad move or not, but Gus didn't seem affected. He pressed his lips together and sighed through his nose. "Do more?"

"I'd like to meet him. Get a chance to prove myself."

Gus shook his head. "These things have never been allowed. Ramón said this is okay?"

Had to make a split second decision. Admit that I had gone over Ramón's head, or lie about it. Either way had serious consequences, but I couldn't back out now.

I chose the lie and nodded.

Gus chewed on his lip for a few seconds, eyeing me. If he said no, I didn't know what I would do. I couldn't go to Ramón and ask him—not that Ramón would have ever said *yes* to that proposition.

Gus reached out and gripped my shoulder, sighing as he bored deep into my eyes. "You have been a good worker, Michael. Very loyal and dependable. You have been with us longer than most."

"Thank you."

"You have earned your spot in the family. But, I'm afraid I cannot allow you to meet El Lobo. It is not something that is done. I hope you understand."

My heart sank. Didn't think I could respond. I averted my eyes so he wouldn't read my expression, and I let him see my head bob up and down as a nod.

"Do not worry, Michael. There will be other opportunities for you. Now, if you'll excuse me, I have to go."

"Do you mind if I use your bathroom?"

His eyes darted to the left, then he nodded. "Certainly. Hank can show you out when you are finished."

I thanked him, and he left me there, broken and defeated. I wished I'd brought the flask inside now, but it didn't matter. I still had to drive across town to meet Pug after this.

My feet felt heavy as I ambled down the hallway to the bathroom. I wanted to splash some water on my face and tell myself that it wasn't all as hopeless as it seemed. Maybe ask Boba Fett to give me a pep talk.

But I didn't make it all the way to the bathroom, because, from an open door on the left emerged Ramón.

CHAPTER FOURTEEN

RAMÓN'S FIERY EYES shot imaginary laser beams at me. "What are you doing here?"

Instead of his customary robe, he was actually dressed. I rarely saw Ramón outside of his apartment, and this had been the second time in two days. I was briefly thrown by the suit and tie he was wearing. He could have been a banker, were it not for the weed/cocaine mixture of both bloodshot eyes.

"I, uh."

"Phillip told me you two were going to drive out into the woods and practice shooting today."

"Yeah, I'm meeting Pug later."

"No one said anything about you coming to Gustavo's house."

"They didn't?"

He got in my face. Weed on his breath. "Stop being

cute. I heard all of it, you little shit. I said it was okay for you to meet El Lobo? Why the hell would I do that?"

I shook my head, desperately trying to think of something clever to say. "No, that's not what I meant. It was a miscommunication. I didn't tell him you said that."

"Are you saying Gustavo isn't smart enough to understand your English?"

I couldn't win with this guy. He leaned even closer to me. Standing only three inches away from him, I could literally feel the heat emanating from his body.

"No, of course not. I wouldn't say that."

"Then why are you here?"

I had nothing. It's not like I could pitch him some story that Gus and I were planning a surprise birthday party for Ramón or something like that. I didn't even know when this chubby bastard's birthday was.

All I could do was shrug.

"Answer me," he said, snarling through gritted teeth.

"I wanted to see if he had any work for me," I said, spitting out the first thing I could think of. "Trying to move up. I wanted to impress him."

Ramón balled his fist but didn't strike me. "Why not come to me first?"

"I assumed you would say no without giving me a chance. And I thought if I talked to Gustavo directly, you would respect me for taking initiative."

"Initiative," Ramón said. "You want more work, you

come see me, understand? You are never to speak to Gustavo again unless I permit it."

Ramón could fire me. If Ramón banned me from the Sinaloa, I wouldn't get my WitSec deal. No WitSec deal and I would be arrested and imprisoned with the rest of them.

To hell with all that, Ramón could have me killed long before I had to worry about any of that garbage.

"You listening, McBriar?"

My mouth dropped open, and I tried to reply, but only air leaked out.

He grabbed me by the shirt, and I had an urge to wrap my hand around his throat and squeeze until the life drained out of his fat, stupid face. To burn the whole situation to the ground. I spent a split second debating if spending my life in prison for murder would be worth extinguishing Ramón.

No, of course, it wasn't. He wasn't worth spending a single day in jail.

Through gritted teeth, he said, "tell me you understand."

"Yes, Ramón, I understand."

Pug squeezed the trigger and the glass bottle exploded into a thousand shards. I watched them settle into the tall grass like fluttering diamonds. We were standing far enough away that I didn't worry about pieces coming anywhere close to us.

I raised my Beretta and tried to aim at the next Coke bottle, perched on the edge of a barrel in this field outside of the city. My eyes had trouble focusing. All three of the remaining bottles blurred together, and as my finger hovered over the trigger, I struggled to connect my brain to my finger and make it squeeze.

"Son of a bitch," I said, and sighed. Tried aiming with my other eye, but that didn't help either. Pug crossed his arms and tilted his head, staring at me.

I couldn't stop thinking about Ramón snarling at me at the top of Gustavo's staircase. The raw vehemence in his eyes at the prospect that I would defy him. Ramón had always been an asshole, but these last few months, he'd morphed into an outright demon.

I'd blown my opportunity with Gus, and now I feared Ramón would make sure I never got anywhere near El Lobo. Not only that, but if the feds discovered that Ramón was suspicious of me, they might yank the deal anyway.

Would the feds know about it, though? Did they have bugs in Gustavo's house or had they already turned some of his guards? It's not like they would tell me if they had.

I hated to be dependent on sketchy Agent Delfino and her promises of WitSec. Hated that I couldn't tell Pug what was going on with me. All of these variables weighed on me ten times as heavily because I had to keep this secret bottled up inside.

"You going to shoot, or what?" Pug said.

I lowered the pistol. "I'm not feeling it today."

"Yeah, no kidding. You've been weirded-out for days now. Is it still about the cop?"

Couldn't argue with that, but I had to say something. "No. I mean, yes, but not really. I haven't really been thinking about the cop. I've managed to mute that part of my brain."

"So what is it?"

"You know that bartender in Stillwater I told you about? The hot one at Willie's?"

Pug holstered his pistol and dug his thumbs into his pockets. "Go on."

"She turned me down."

"So what?"

I shrugged. "I know it shouldn't be a big deal. I've just been after her for a long time."

"Two things I know for sure, Mikey: until they give me cancer, the only cigarettes worth smoking are Parliaments. And second, there are many fishy fish in the sea."

I nodded, didn't want to lie to him anymore by continuing this conversation. I mean, yes, obviously, Krista giving me the cold shoulder sucked, but it was fairly low on the priority list right now.

A little voice inside my head told me to come out with the truth. To tell Pug everything. But I couldn't do that. I had to get this WitSec deal.

My brain felt like a war zone. Two sides, constantly lobbing grenades at each other.

Why couldn't I come clean with my best friend? Why was I valuing the word of the federal government over this person who'd been at my side for years?

Because I was weak, that's why. Because I still thought I could protect him, even though that prospect was iffy at best. At worst, I'd be responsible for sending him to prison for the rest of his life.

"If you're looking to get laid," Pug said. "I can set you up with someone. I met the perfect girl the other night, the kind with just the right level of questionable morals. She was all over me until I explained to her that she was fishing in the wrong pond. She would be totally down for a no-strings booty call."

"Thanks, but that's not what I'm looking for."

"Is there something you're not telling me?" he said. "Whatever it is, Mike, you know you can say it."

"I had a bad run-in with Ramón earlier today. Rattled me a little."

"Ahh," he said, spreading a knowing smile. "I get it.

To Ramón, getting under your skin is like crafting a beautiful portrait or composing a sonnet. What was it about?"

"I wanted to meet El Lobo when he comes into town this weekend. Ramón shot me down."

"Why would you want to meet him?"

Only then did I realize that giving Pug that information had been a mistake. Because I'd told the truth, my only option was to lie to cover it up. I couldn't come up with a good answer, so I shrugged and mumbled something noncommittal. When Pug could see I wasn't going to reveal any details, he left it alone.

I walked toward the remainder of our target practice bottles. Pug followed, and we checked the barrel for bullet holes. He dropped to one knee and picked at a hole in the side of the barrel. "Those redneck crack-heads we messed with in Sand Springs? If they're coming back for retribution, we have to keep our heads down and be smart. We need to do everything we can to stay alive by watching each other's backs. It's dumb to trust anyone else to do that for us."

"I know."

"Please don't disappear on me anymore, Mike."

"I understand," I said.

He nodded and collected the unbroken glass bottles, cradling them in the crook of his arm.

"Speaking of disappearing," I said, "I was thinking

about what they did to that kid at the warehouse yesterday. The one who came back for his sick mom."

Pug blew out a sigh through pursed lips. "Yeah, that was hard to watch. What was he thinking, though? He took off without a word, and then shows up years later? He had to know it was a terrible risk."

"I've been wondering if maybe he had Witness Protection or something."

Pug's head cocked slightly. "Witness Protection?"

"Yeah. I mean, how else would someone get away from the Sinaloa?"

"Nobody gets away from the Sinaloa, Mikey. Not alive, anyway."

CHAPTER FIFTEEN

SINCE PUG AND I had spent most of the evening together in and near Oklahoma City, I decided not to make the hour-long slog back to Stillwater. My body ached in multiple places and today had dragged on forever. I did have a room at the Freedom House, although I didn't like to stay there. Cinderblock walls and no air conditioning.

But before I could get some sleep, I had an idea to explore first. I kept thinking back to my meeting with Gus that morning, the business card with the raised image of the wolf's head.

One time, about a year ago, some beefy white guy with long hair and a beard had strolled into a meeting at a bar in the OKC suburb of Moore. Ramón had been trying to negotiate something with the bartender. The details were fuzzy; I'd been quite drunk that day. But I definitely recalled Ramón's affronted reaction to that guy when he strutted in and inserted himself into the conversation. I thought Ramón was going to shoot him on the spot. But then, the guy pulled out a copy of that wolf business card, and Ramón shut right up. Let the guy take over the dealings with the bartender. I'd never seen Ramón cower to anyone except Gus before.

If I had one of those cards, maybe I could walk right up to El Lobo and introduce myself. Maybe I could treat it as a universal key to unlock whatever doors I wanted.

I'd also overheard Ramón telling someone that El Lobo was coming to Dallas in two days, his last stop before visiting Oklahoma City. Maybe I didn't even need to wait for this OKC meeting. I could get to Lobo there, and it wouldn't have to involve Gus, or Ramón, or even Pug. I could flash that card and earn a seat at the table, and no one in Oklahoma City would have to know anything about it.

The perfect ruse to get what I wanted.

I just had to find a way to acquire one of those cards, and the things were prized possessions. Their owners didn't leave them lying around.

But, I knew Gus kept one in his wallet, so I had an idea where to start. If I infiltrated late enough, after he went to sleep, I could assume his wallet would be in his bedroom. I'd been in that room once at a party when I'd been given the grand responsibility of managing everyone's coats.

That day, I spent some time sitting in Gus' bedroom during my coat-managing duties. Breathing in the materialism of it all. He had one of those curved TV screens so big that it made going out to the movies pointless. Back then, I'd entertained fantasies of having the same setup someday, after I'd made my fortune. My trophy wife and I would retire each night to our leather recliners and watch first-run movies while serfs fed us grapes from golden dishes and fanned us with giant leaves.

Forget the serfs and the trophy wife. Things had turned out a bit differently for me, and now I needed to survive.

All I had to do was break into his heavily-guarded Nichols Hills mansion, evade his surveillance cameras, get past his ample security, sneak into his bedroom, steal the card, and then escape without anyone seeing me.

No problem. No problem at all.

So I sat in my Jeep, sipping at my flask with Gus' mansion off in the distance, waiting for the sun to set. I took Boba Fett from my pocket and set him on the dashboard.

"Think we can do this?"

Hell yeah, we can do this, Boba said.

"I appreciate the vote of confidence."

Don't get too drunk, though.

I sipped from my flask again. "I'm fine. I'll keep it together."

Once you commit, you commit. There's no turning back when you go down this road.

"I get it. This has to happen."

I popped open the glove box, hid my flask, and had to make a choice between the Beretta and my hunting knife. If I found myself in a situation where I was going to have to use either, I'd probably have already passed the point of no return. But, I figured, I might get in less trouble with the knife. I could maybe explain my presence. If caught with a gun in my hand inside Gus's house, there wouldn't be any clever words or diversions that could prevent my death sentence. So I chose the knife, even though it might not do much good. With that and my lock picking kit, I was good to go.

I'd parked far enough away that I didn't worry about my car getting me in trouble, and I skirted the sidewalk until I met the edge of the security cameras' range. There would be one for sure at the front gate, and probably some lining the fence around the property.

A dog, something sleek and black with a white patch on its chest, ambled down the sidewalk toward me. Muscular, with floppy ears and drooping jowls.

"Hey boy," I said as I dropped to one knee.

The dog's tail wagged as it padded closer to me. Pit bull.

I held out a hand, and it sniffed my fingers, then its mouth dropped open and it peered up at me, panting.

"I know, it's hot out here tonight, right?"

The dog sat, his head slightly tilted. Stared.

"You have a home?" I said as I noticed the dog wasn't wearing a collar.

The dog didn't say anything, so I patted it on the head. "Well, if the dog catcher comes around looking for you, I won't say a word. And if they do pick you up, you keep your mouth shut too, and ask for a lawyer. If they offer you a deal, it's probably bullshit."

I hopped the neighbor's fence and looked back at the dog, who now seemed confused. Maybe he thought I'd take him home with me, but I wasn't going to be in the business of taking on new dependents anytime soon.

The neighbor's house was as large as Gustavo's, set back from the road, with rolling green hills blanketing the house on all sides. I wondered if this guy had any idea what next-door Gus Salazar did for a living.

I walked away from the fence line a few hundred feet, watching Gus' tall wrought iron fence, looking for cameras. Every so often, the wrought iron bars met at brick pillars, and I studied those, looking for little red lights or the reflection of glass. I didn't see anything worth mentioning. If I ventured much further into the neighbor's yard, I would run the risk of being spotted by someone at that house. Instead, I veered toward Gus' fence.

Still couldn't see any cameras. Maybe with all the security at the house, Gus only had them installed on the front, near the entry gate.

Pug's words from this afternoon repeated in my head. *No one gets away from the Sinaloa.* But then why was he saving all that money to buy the land in Maud? Was that a pipe dream, and Pug didn't actually expect to get away someday?

Couldn't think about that now.

I climbed up one of those brick pillars and dropped on the other side. Maybe two hundred yards from the house. It stood three stories, with second and third-floor balconies that wrapped around the back and sides of the house. I sat in the grass under a tree with the chirping crickets and frogs and spent thirty minutes studying these balconies. I counted two security guards working on a rotation approximately six times an hour, coming out one door and then rounding the balcony.

So I had to time my approach in between their rotations, which wasn't too challenging. I would have a few minutes to accomplish that. The real problem was the cameras on the outskirts, the small black orbs protruding from the side of the house every thirty feet or so. I wouldn't be able to tell which way the cameras inside those orbs were pointing. And since there was no tunnel into the basement, seems I was shit out of luck for an approach that would avoid them.

I'd have to gamble that no one was actively watching those camera feeds.

Once I'd entered the house, I would have to hurry to find the card. If Gus hadn't stashed it somewhere, that would mean it would be in his wallet. His wallet would be in his back pocket, which meant I needed to wait until he went to sleep.

Checked the time on my phone. 9:00 pm.

I set an alarm on my phone and snuggled up to the tree for a nap.

My pocket buzzed, and I awoke with a start. I yanked out my phone and thumbed the button to turn off the alarm. 1:00 in the morning. If Gus wasn't asleep by now, I didn't know what I would do. Wait longer, I guess.

I studied the house for another half hour and noticed the guard balcony sweep frequency had softened. That was good. I didn't see any lights flicking on or off inside the house, but it was hard to tell because of the exterior fog lights illuminating the nearby ground.

He was probably asleep. Probably.

Time to go for it.

I silenced my phone and waited until the security guard made one more sweep along the balcony. Had plenty of time to move without being seen from above, unless one of them made some unscheduled trip. Despite that possibility, I didn't have a better time than right now.

I set my sights on the back door and sprinted across the yard, straight for it. Even with my jeans and black t-shirt, I wouldn't be invisible. I had to hope that I would only be within the reach of those fog lights for a second or two.

The back of the house led out to a deck with chairs and tables, then a concrete area around a jacuzzi and a swimming pool. Past that, a gazebo and a bunch of other fancy crap like hedge sculptures of lions. Had to stop from gawking at the luxuriousness of it all. I wondered what El Lobo's house looked like. He probably lived in a castle on a Mexican hillside.

Approaching from the side of the deck, I wouldn't have to worry about those well-lit areas. I could plot a path past the initial wide fog lights and creep to the side of the deck across a small sliver of grass outside the lights' reach.

But I had to consider another wrinkle if I was going to approach the back door that way: Gus' dogs. His two humongous Dobermans lived in a large cage near the back porch. I'd met them before, and they'd seemed friendly enough. But maybe not if I was streaking across the yard in the dark of night.

I glanced toward the kennel and saw both of them

prone on blankets, heads down and sleeping. Skirting by them was my best option.

Time to move.

As I crossed the beam of a fog light, one of the dogs lifted his head, tilted it and sniffed, but didn't bark. I tried not to meet the dog's eyes because somebody told me once that's a sign of aggression.

Good doggie. No bark. Let this stranger rob your daddy. Seemed like all the dogs I'd met tonight were on my side.

I hit the back deck and wrestled my lock picking kit out of my pocket as I crouched in front of the door. Pressed my ear against it, and nothing but silence came back. No vibrations. If I'd been seen on the cameras, I could expect company within seconds.

With the lock pick kit in hand, I breathed for a moment, trying to remember what to do. My hands shook with a slight tremor, probably because I'd slept off what little booze I'd consumed in the car when I'd arrived. And then I wasted another couple of precious seconds being angry at my hand for not holding steady.

You can do this, Boba said, hidden away in my pocket.

I went to work at the lock, using my two angled tools to slip the bolt. Bottom one held the lock in place while I dug around for the pins with the top one. Had it unlocked in thirty seconds, a new personal record. I paused before opening the door, thinking about the possibility of an alarm. I couldn't remember seeing any panels next to the front door. Maybe with the security cameras and the armed thugs patrolling, Gus didn't think he needed one.

I opened the door.

No alarm blared.

Inside, a dark utility room glared back at me. Washer and dryer to my left. Shelves on the right stuffed high with towels and dog food bags. On the wall next to the shelves: a framed drawing, probably drawn by a little kid. A handprint with swirls of crayon all around it and an illegible name scrawled at the bottom.

For a second, I thought I might get lucky enough to find the card in his dirty laundry. But that was a no-go. This room had zero pants scattered among the other dirty clothes. No, he'd have his wallet with the card near him. I would have to sneak into his room, probably find the pants in a laundry bin and his wallet on the night-stand next to him.

I'd have to pilfer that wallet, inches away from Gustavo's sleeping head. But that was a problem to worry about in a few minutes. I had to get to his room first.

I crept to the other end of the small laundry room and perched next to the closed door. Pressed my ear against it. This time, I could hear some vibration and a rumbling sound come back. Could have been the air conditioner. I stilled my breathing and tried to hear variations, but the sounds were all level, as far as I could tell. Definitely air conditioner.

I creaked open the door to a hallway lit by one lamp. Dim. I recognized the hallway because it led out to the main entry room of the house with the marble stairs and the extravagant chandelier. I didn't want to stroll up the main stairs if I could help it. There would be minimal cover out there in the main room.

I needed to look for a back stairway around here somewhere. In a house this big, there had to be at least one.

I checked the first door on the left, which opened to a bathroom. Caught my reflection in the mirror, had a moment to appreciate how ragged I looked. I hadn't been sleeping well for weeks, and I'd spent even less time admiring myself in mirrors. The bags under my eyes were like the anti-glare smears football players wear as war paint on their cheeks. My hair was matted and unkempt since I hadn't been to a barber in three or four months.

I closed the door and tried not to think about it. Maybe once I was beyond all this, living a new life in Witness Protection in Hawaii or Southern California, I'd go to rehab so I could emerge all clean and healthy looking. Get a tan and drink vitamin-laced electrolyte drinks like Pug.

But first, I had to live long enough to make that happen.

I listened at the door to my right and heard nothing. Slipped it open to find an office room with a paper-cluttered desk, some bookshelves, and a standing globe.

Next to one of the bookshelves sat a bar with a collection of half-full bottles, every color of the rainbow. Like a drunkard's wet dream there, ripe for the taking.

My mouth watered. Stopping for a drink of Gus' liquor would be pure insanity. I knew how often one drink turned into two or three, and closed my eyes to break the thought train.

But, my throat was terribly dry.

No, Boba Fett warned me from inside my pocket. *Stop to drink, you'll get caught. Don't do it.*

"Fine," I whispered to the room.

I peeked back into the hallway and then shut the door behind me. Slipped a little further down toward the entry room with the chandelier, keeping close to the wall and letting my feet float onto the floor with each step. Only one more door up ahead on the right to investigate. If that didn't yield anything, I'd have no choice but to cross the fully-lit entryway, where anyone at the top of those stairs could spot me.

And while I was thinking about that, footsteps came clomping down the stairs. Not measured steps, but someone running, taking them two or three at a time.

I panicked. Raced forward, navigated around a wooden chair next to the last door, and threw it open to find a dark closet. I jumped inside and closed the door, having to resist the urge to slam it shut. Coats on hangars swayed behind me. Shoes bumped up against my feet.

I seized the knob with one hand, trying to get my racing heart under control. Arm shaking. Jaw tensed. Head swimming.

The footsteps slowed and proceeded into the hallway. I eased the knife from my pocket with the other hand and pointed the tip at the door. If I had to stab someone, this quiet infiltration would probably end soon after. That didn't mean I wouldn't do it if necessary.

Oh God, please don't let this person open the door. My life and Pug's life and everything right now hung on this one little stupid hope. How insane was all this? I couldn't get over the fact that all of this was not a dream.

I glanced down at the light filtering under the door from the hallway. Two shadows cut through the light and then paused outside the closet. Feet.

A walkie-talkie squawked. A voice came on, said something in Spanish I couldn't understand. You'd think in the last few years I might have learned more of it. Hadn't ever been a priority. Now I wished I'd made it one.

Another voice came back over the walkie, in English.

"If it's quiet, it's quiet. Don't run down the stairs like that again. If you wake him up, it'll be your ass."

Good news: Gus was asleep upstairs. Bad news: if the man in the hallway opened this door, it wouldn't matter where Gus was.

The guard standing outside the closet mumbled something else in Spanish, and then the hallway went quiet. The foot-shadows didn't move.

My pulse still raced, and I focused all of my energy on breathing normally. I held the tip of the knife against the inside of the door, at about the same level as my throat. If he opened the door, I'd jab him in the neck and pull his body inside the closet as quickly as possible. I had to guess where this guy's throat-level would be.

The feet moved, and then my heart sank when I heard the creak of wood outside the door. He'd sat in the chair next to the door.

Shit.

I let go of the doorknob because my hand was so sweaty it wouldn't have done me any good to try to keep it shut. I closed my eyes for a minute, desperately scheming my next move. What if he took a little nap out there? It was the middle of the night, after all. Maybe if he slept, I could sneak out past him. But unless he started snoring, I'd have no way to know.

My knees wobbled, so I crouched down. Had to get out of this space, but digging a hole in the floor wasn't exactly an option. Now I wished I hadn't left my flask in the car.

I finally opened my eyes, and they'd now adjusted to the darkness, I could see the full range of coats and scarves and other things hanging around me. Beyond that, the back wall of the closet. And there I found my salvation: a hinge on the back wall.

CHAPTER SIXTEEN

I REACHED OUT to the back wall of the closet and fingered the hinge nearest to the top. Found another halfway down the wall, and a third near the floor. This back wall of this closet wasn't a wall, it was a secret door.

I traced my hands to the other side, careful not to move the jackets hanging from the hangars in front of me. Found a slit in the wall running from floor to ceiling. No door handle or grip, though. I pressed on the side opposite the hinges, and it depressed a fraction of an inch, clicked, and then popped back toward me a couple inches. This door-like thing must have been sealed with magnets, like glass enclosures on cabinets. Chilled air rushed in when I opened it a little wider.

I definitely planned to buy a house with secret doors

someday. If I weren't so mind-numbingly anxious, I would have been astounded by how cool this was.

I took a few of the jackets on hangers and carefully placed them on the side closest to the hinge so I could create a pathway. I reached into the open crack made by the door and pulled it back toward me, creating enough space to fit my body through the door.

Sucking in a breath, I eased inside the secret door and found myself staring at a pitch black room or hallway or something. I stepped into it and closed the door behind me. It clicked as I shut it.

Red lights flicked on behind me.

I spun, frantic, until I realized the lights above had been triggered from motion sensors. I was standing in a short hallway, and I was the only person here. Just a set of stairs on the left. I turned on my flashlight, holding it low just in case.

I wasn't surprised that Gus had a secret room. I kinda expected rich people to have these sorts of things, in addition to having garages built to hold only their motorcycles, wine cellars, and stables for horses they'd never meet.

The walls were covered with art, stuff that was like paint splotches made by a drunk person with an aggressive paintbrush. Not my scene. I liked pictures of sunsets and mountains and all that normal junk. Abstract stuff was way beyond my brain capacity.

A grate had been nailed to one little section of the

wall, with guns hanging from hooks along the grate. Pistols, shotguns, machine guns. Pristine high-end guns and rifles.

An urge burned at me to pull one of those shotguns off the walls and hunt around for some shells. But if I had to shoot up the place, I might as well let them catch me. I'd possibly live out the night long enough to flee Oklahoma City, but I'd be dead within a few hours of escaping this house. No doubt.

And the person who would hunt me down and put a bullet in me would be someone who looked just like me. Another lost kid following orders.

So I left the guns where I found them and slinked up the stairs, careful to lower each foot slowly until I'd set my full weight on it. These stairs didn't creak, though. Little lights ran along the underside of the steps, like in a movie theater.

Twenty steps up, the stairs turned a corner, and there was a door at a small landing. I leaned near it, listening. Could hear voices on the other side. I had no idea where this secret door let out to. Hallways? Bedrooms? No way to know without taking that plunge.

I resumed my stair climbing since I knew Gus' bedroom was on the third floor. At the next landing, I found a door with a simple handle sticking out from it. Listened, heard nothing but the rumble of air conditioning vibrating the wood.

Third floor. The stairs ended here, so I didn't have much choice other than to open this door. The hinges were on the inside facing me, so I pulled at the handle, a quarter of an inch.

Before I opened it any more, I considered the escape route. If I returned back down the stairs, I might find that Spanish-speaking guard still sitting in the chair outside the closet. If that didn't pan out, I'd probably have to go down the house's front stairs, in the fully-lit entry room. Secret route sounded like the best way, napping guard or not.

I peeked through to darkness inside. I opened it a little more until a bed came into view. I leaned my head through the opening, saw that same megalithic television hanging from the wall opposite two plush leather recliners.

Gus' bedroom. I'd caught a break, finally. The lights were off, and two shapes ballooned the covers of the bed. Gus and his wife. This room was about ten degrees colder than the rest of the house, which explained why they were nestled under a down comforter in the middle of July.

I took the knife from my pocket again, gripped the hilt. If they woke up, I'd be dead before I could talk my way out of this. I'd have to kill them both and pray I could do so quietly.

Gus? I could end him with no problem. Even though he'd always been decent to me, I knew what a monster he was at heart. I'd once seen Gus drive an icepick through the foot of a man who'd been suspected of stealing, and then Gus beat the man with a sock full of ball bearings while he was pinned to the ground. Hadn't even been proved to be a thief; only a suspected one.

But his wife? The mother of his children? She hadn't done anything wrong. Would I be able to plunge this knife into her chest, if it came down to my life or hers? I didn't think I could do it. I prayed that I wouldn't have to do it. So far, the two people I'd killed had been trying to kill me. They had been bad people, as far as I could tell. Killing an innocent person was a line I didn't know if I could cross.

If I got what I came for and left stealthily, I wouldn't have to find out.

I crept across the room, knife out. Gus snored softly in the bed. He shifted. I froze. A moment later, his snoring continued, and I kept looking around the room, searching for a clothes hamper or a pair of pants discarded on the floor. Nothing jumped out at me.

I circled the bed and checked out his wife's side, found no pants there either. A moment of panic arose when I realized that Gus might keep his wallet in some locked safe at night. Then I glanced across the bed and saw it: that fat crocodile wallet, sitting on his nightstand.

Six inches away from his face.

I returned to his side of the bed and held my breath

as I tiptoed within striking distance of the wallet. My eyes flicked back and forth between his closed eyes and the nightstand. At that wallet, which contained my golden key to gaining access to El Lobo.

I stowed the knife and reached out for the wallet.

And then gunfire erupted outside the house.

CHAPTER SEVENTEEN

AS GUNFIRE ERUPTED somewhere outside the house, I stared in horror down at Gustavo's sleeping face. His eyes weren't yet open.

Shouts came from outside Gus' room. I had to make a decision. I dropped to the floor and scurried under the bed, flattening myself to squeeze into the narrow space between the bed and the plush carpet.

The door flew open, and I had to hope that my feet weren't dangling out from the edge. The room lights flicked on and the bed shifted above me. Someone in the bed must have sat up, because the box springs pressed down, stealing my breath. I did my best not to gulp air back in.

"Gustavo," said a harried and winded voice. After a moment, I recognized it as Hank's, the guy who'd let me in the house the other day.

The rattle of gunfire continued in sporadic bursts from outside.

"What's going on?" asked a female voice. Gus' wife. I'd only met her once, and I couldn't think of her name. She had mixed me a wickedly strong margarita. I remembered that much.

"Ma'am, some people are at the house, shooting at us."

"Are they over the gate?" Gus said.

Hank didn't respond, so he must have nodded. Gus whipped back the covers and hopped out of bed. I took a full breath now that the weight was off me.

"Get her to the safe room," Gus said. I heard a belt buckle clink as he slipped on his pants.

"I want to stay with you," she said.

"Go with Hank," Gus growled. "I'll get the kids."

The fact that Gus was going to put himself in danger to save his children almost made me feel guilty that I was willing to stab him to death a few seconds ago. Then, I remembered the guy he'd beaten with the sock full of ball bearings, and the guilt evaporated.

Footsteps thundered across the carpet, and now I could hear people in the house shouting and running.

I held my breath. In another moment, a door slammed behind me. I craned my neck to look. The lights were still on, but the room had quieted. Outside the room was the chaos of running and shouting and blasts from semiautomatic rifles, but Gus' room felt oddly still.

I pushed myself out from underneath the bed and rose to my feet. Commotion outside the room became like the whirring drone of a fan.

I had to get out of here. Whatever this drama was, I couldn't be caught here. With all these people coming and going, someone was going to check this room.

But then, out of the corner of my eye, I noticed Gus' wallet, still sitting on the nightstand. I snatched it and flicked through it. Cash, license, library card, credit cards, dozens of paper receipts nestled inside.

But no wolf card.

"Are you shitting me?" I said to the room.

Didn't matter. I had to go. I flipped the wallet back onto the nightstand and drew my knife as I approached the entrance to the hidden staircase. There was a crease in the wall, and I pressed on it, which slid the door open a fraction. I paused with my hand on the edge of the door. If I found one of these attackers, I'd have to kill him. If I found Gus' men, they'd probably assume I was involved in this raid, and I'd have to kill them too.

I didn't want to kill anybody.

With a grunt, I threw back the door to the darkened stairwell. Hustled down the stairs to the first floor, now noticing several of the guns on the rack gone. I snatched a shotgun and stowed my knife.

Mossberg 500 Tactical, fully loaded. It looked and

smelled so clean that it had to be brand new. I'd read about these but had never fired one. After cocking it, I opened the door into the closet, then leaned against the door into the hallway and listened. I could still hear gunfire outside, but nothing out in the hallway. The guy in the chair couldn't still be snoozing out there. No way.

I threw open the door and jumped out into the hallway. Empty.

I raced down the hall toward the laundry room, intending to go out the way I'd come in. Pulled the laundry room door closed behind me and paused to catch my breath. My heart was thumping so fast I couldn't seem to get ahead of it. My stomach gurgled, and I had an overpowering desire to sit and close my eyes.

No. Time to go. I yanked open the exterior door to find a face just two feet from my own.

Young person standing opposite me, right outside the door, with a submachine gun hanging from a strap. His hand was out, reaching for the knob. Utter surprise on his face. His gun wasn't in his hands, it was hanging loosely on the strap, next to his hip.

For a moment, nothing happened. We just looked at each other. This kid was about my same age, but I could see the years of drug abuse as bags lining his eyes and pale skin rough from acne and apathy. Did I look like that?

The kid blinked and scrambled to control his submachine gun.

I raised the shotgun and pulled the trigger. The Mossberg roared like a lion in my hands. The intruder flew back as his midsection turned into a red mess and chunks of him spread in all directions. He bumped into a deck chair. Folded backward over it.

The recoil from the shotgun made me stumble back, and I bumped into the washer. I looked around, dazed, vision blurry. The handprint drawing on the wall smiled back at me.

I dropped the shotgun and fled the house. The crackhead fell from the chair onto the deck, writhing, not quite dead yet. Couldn't believe I'd torn a person apart like that. He had to know that his guts were spilling out of him, with only seconds to live.

How would that feel? I couldn't even imagine it.

But this assailant, this crackhead, he was going to kill me. He would have put a bullet in me just as easily if he'd had the chance.

And judging by the fact that a crackhead was here, our little skirmish on the bridge yesterday had indeed started a war. Just as Pug had predicted it would. Just as Gus and Ramón had wanted.

Maybe they hadn't predicted an assault this ballsy. Gus' house was like an armed fortress.

I didn't care about any of that, though. I had my

sights on the fence, to one of those brick pillars. From there, the neighbor's yard, and my car, and home.

I didn't go straight home, even though that had been my first instinct. No, I sped out of the neighborhood and hit I-44, then drove two more miles until I found a turnoff with a QuikTrip gas station. My car crawled into the parking lot like a wounded animal seeking a quiet cave for rest.

I gripped the steering wheel until my hands ached. The world around me filtered in and out, sometimes there, sometimes imaginary.

On one side of my car sat a gleaming Lexus, on the other, a ratty old Honda Accord. Both of the cars had wheels, tires, seats, headlights. My sturdy Jeep sat sandwiched between them. For the life of me, I couldn't figure out why I was paying attention to the cars on either side of mine.

I reached for the flask and had a sip… just a sip, because I still had to drive. I was going home tonight, no matter what. Away from this craziness.

A man in a dress shirt and tie exited the QuikTrip, phone in one hand and keys in the other. He headed in my direction, and I didn't have to think hard about whether he was going to choose the old Honda or the shiny new Lexus. His shoes looked more expensive than my rent. What was he doing here at QuickTrip in the middle of the night? Slumming it to buy condoms for a visit to his mistress? Getting a pack of gum to wash the taste of cigars out of his mouth after a late night gambling away his kid's college fund?

The posh man frowned at me as he chirped the car unlock on his Lexus and slipped inside the car. He thought he knew me, based on one glance walking out of a convenience store. Whatever.

I wanted so badly to call Pug and tell him everything that had happened, but I knew I couldn't. Shouldn't. I wouldn't be able to explain to him even how I'd known about the crackheads' raid on Gus' house.

Maybe I should have stuck around after all that to see how it had ended. Gus and his family might not have survived the assault. If he died, would that interfere with my WitSec deal? Would it make El Lobo reconsider his trip to Oklahoma City?

An hour passed, me sitting in that parking lot, watching people enter and exit the convenience store. Buying cigarettes, beer, energy drinks. Once I'd calmed down, I got back on the highway and headed home. The night sky began to lighten, and by the time I neared Stillwater, the sun had started to climb over the trees to the east.

I had a six pack of Bud Light in the fridge, and I resolved to pound all six of them, sleep for two days, and then figure out what the hell I was supposed to do next.

Except when I finally made it back to my apartment and climbed the rickety wooden stairs, I found Special Agent Delfino sitting on the walkway outside my apartment. A baseball cap pulled low, sweatshirt, jeans.

"Hi, Michael. Want to let me in?"

I gritted my teeth, then opened my flask and drained it. "Why didn't you let yourself in?"

She stood and wiped off the back of her pants. She didn't answer me, instead flicked her head at the door. Impatient scowl on her face.

"Fine," I said as I palmed my keys. My hand shook as I tried to unlock the door. Had three failed attempts. I could feel Delfino's eyes boring into the back of my head, judging me.

She glared at my fumbling. "You okay?"

I finally got the door unlocked and waved her in. I opened the fridge and removed the whole six pack of Bud, then sat in the Papasan chair with the beer in my lap. I opened the first and swallowed half in two gulps. Enjoyed a momentary victory of being alive, in my favorite chair, with a cold beverage wetting my throat.

Delfino perched on the milk crate across from me. Rubbed her hands together.

"Am I going to see you every day now?" I said. "People will say we're in love. I have a reputation around the building to uphold, you know."

"You mean you and your downstairs neighbor? I saw him the other day. Pretty sure he's too high to know who you are."

I sighed. "Fine. It's not even six o'clock in the morning. What do you want?"

She reached into her sweatshirt and withdrew an envelope, just like the one she'd used to show me those incriminating pictures back in that interrogation room. Except this time, she opened the flap and removed a pack of stapled papers.

"What's that?"

"Your deal," she said. "I got approval late last night. Witness Protection, contingent upon providing evidence and testimony against Luis Velasquez and other members of the Sinaloa cartel."

"Contingent upon?"

"There are no free rides in this life."

I stared at the envelope and the papers in her hands. With some signatures from the right people on those documents, I could become someone else. Leave all of this behind. I had some horrible burdens to endure first, but on the other side of that fuss, I would get my clean slate. I'd flee from the Sinaloa and never have to do awful things I didn't want to so I could pay the rent.

A new life as a new person. New social security card. New drivers license. A new name.

"Do I get to pick my name, or are they going to assign me something I'll hate, like Ralph?"

"Sometimes, people keep their first name. But you'll work all that out with the US Marshals. They're the ones who get you set up somewhere else, with new paperwork and all that. Once you're passed off to them, you'll never see me again. That's for everyone's protection."

I set the six pack on the floor and leaned forward. "Immunity?"

She shook her head. "You'll probably have to do some time, but not much, and not in a regular prison. Protective Custody."

"How does that work?"

"Some prisons have blocks that are segregated from the general population. You'll be with others in WitSec, most likely. I've heard it's not nearly as bad as doing regular time."

She held the stack of papers out to me, and I reached for them, but she pulled them back at the last second.

"But there's a problem," she said.

Of course. I detested this game because I'd played it before, too. Dangle the carrot, yank it back. "What problem?"

"You may not know that there was an attack on one of your boss' houses early this morning, about four hours ago. Some kind of turf war."

I averted my eyes, but I hadn't meant to. It had happened automatically, and I cursed myself because my *tell* had been so damn obvious.

"Hmm," she said. "Or maybe you do know. Either way, this complicates things. We don't know if Velasquez will keep his meeting on Sunday."

"That's still four days away. He'll come."

"If he doesn't, you'll have to think of something else. No meeting, no deal."

My vision blurred with anger. She was going to tease this deal and then hold it back? "What are you saying? What do I do? Why don't you people help me?"

She shrugged. "You're just a piece of the puzzle."

"What does that mean?"

"It's better if you don't know. This needs to be handled organically, Michael. It's important, for procedural reasons I can't go into."

"So I get into a room with him or the deal's off?"

She lifted her palm toward the ceiling, and for some reason, it irked me. "If you don't get both yourself and Luis Velasquez on the same recording, then I can't promise you anything."

"This is such bullshit. You're setting me up for failure."

She frowned at the six pack at my feet, now half finished. "I think you're doing a good enough job of that on your own. Maybe coming to you was a waste of time."

I glanced at the papers again. I loathed the way this woman played me like a guitar, but those documents held so much promise for me. They were everything.

I had to do whatever I could.

"I'm not a waste of time. I can do this."

She stood and dropped the stack of papers at my feet. "We'll see. Get some sleep. You look like hell."

As the door closed behind her, I stared down at my possible future on the floor and cracked another beer.

CHAPTER EIGHTEEN

PUG'S GLOVED FIST sailed into my stomach, and I felt a momentary pang of relief that I hadn't eaten anything yet. I didn't even want to be here, in this dingy boxing gym in Stillwater. Pug was the morning person, not me. But, if I wanted to hang out with him, this was the price I had to pay, even on two hours of sleep.

I stumbled back into the ropes. Pug danced for a second and then spit out his mouthpiece. "This may be the stupidest idea you've ever had."

"Breakfast at Shortcakes?" I said, panting.

"No, Mikey. Breakfast at Shortcakes is a brilliant idea. I'm talking about what you want to do after that."

I glanced around the gym, noted a guy pummeling a heavy bag ten feet outside the ring. I tilted my head toward the guy, and Pug nodded. We exited the ring to the other side.

I leaned close to Pug's ear and whispered, "this is the best plan. We take these guys out, we end this war now. No more losses on our side."

Pug picked at the tape on his gloves. "Since when are you such a believer?"

Couldn't tell him the truth. "We started this war. You and me. If we don't find a way to be the first to end it, then if the crackheads don't kill us, Ramón will."

Pug soured as he stared off into space. "Fucking Ramón."

"I'm a hundred percent on-board with that statement. But you don't want to be out of a job, do you? Have you saved enough yet?"

Pug shook his head. "The owners of the land won't come down anymore. I'm still almost a hundred thousand short."

I did a double-take. "What? Why would that stretch of nothing cost so much?"

"Because," he whispered, still not looking at me, "they think there's oil there. They haven't been able to find it."

"And you know where it is?"

"No," he said, scoffing. "There's no oil. With all that high-tech equipment they have, someone would have found it by now. But what actually *is* there to be found is something much better."

"What?"

Pug pivoted toward me and dropped his boxing gloves on the gym floor. "You ever heard of Clint Blackney?"

"No, should I?"

"Probably not. I guess you'd call him an outlaw. He was friends with my great, great, something-or-other grandfather. Close friends, probably lovers, if you ask me. Anyway, Clint Blackney robbed a train that held the personal possessions of one Andrew Johnson, President of these here United States. Items on the way to Johnson's personal library."

I crossed my arms. "Okay?"

"Johnson's library was supposed to contain hundreds of letters and notes from President Lincoln, but they never made it to their destination. Some of these letters allegedly described how Lincoln had never wanted to free the slaves. Real inflammatory stuff that would blow apart all the history books."

"You're over-selling it, but I'm listening. Go on."

"After Blackney robbed the train, Johnson's stuff never materialized anywhere, ever again. And Blackney was last seen in Guthrie, Oklahoma, a couple days after the robbery."

"And you think these secret letters are buried on your family land."

Pug raised a hand into the air. "Ding ding ding! We

have a winner. Do you have any idea how much money that crap would be worth?"

"I don't, and it sounds like an urban legend."

He shrugged. "I disagree. And once that deed is mine, I can tear up all four hundred of those acres until I find it. I'll be proving you wrong once I'm sipping drinks on a yacht with my pool boy."

"Then it sounds like you have a legit reason to keep working, my dear Pugsley."

"Looks that way."

A sudden uneasy feeling came over me. I'd known Pug for half my life, but he'd never mentioned this before. "Why are you telling me this now?"

Pug averted his eyes, just as I'd done to Agent Delfino a few hours before. Something was going on with him; something not right.

Across the gym, a lunkhead with over-developed deltoids growled like a bear as he tried to flip over a monster truck tire. Half the gym stopped to gawk at him.

"Remind me," Pug said, "why this grand plan?"

Again I fought the urge to tell him the truth. That if Gus and Ramón died and El Lobo avoided Oklahoma City, I'd go to jail for the rest of my life. And if I did that, I'd have no way to protect Pug in court.

I decided to tell him something close to the truth. "Maybe I don't want to see anyone else on our side die."

Pug lifted a water bottle to his lips and sipped some

lime green fluid. That guy was always drinking brain enhancing foo-foo juice. "What happened last night was a mess, that's for sure."

Pug had given me the update earlier, and I'd done my best to act surprised. Most of Gus' security had been killed. Gus, his wife, and his kids survived. There would be a reckoning for that assault, no doubt about it. And if we could get out in front of it and look like heroes, maybe Gus would grant me the audience with Luis Velasquez I'd been seeking. Or, at the least, I could keep Gus alive so he could go to jail with the rest of them.

"Okay," Pug said, sighing, "I'm on board with your clearly-foolhardy and doomed-to-fail idea. But you're buying breakfast."

This was the plan: In Sand Springs, the little meth town within spitting distance of Tulsa proper, there was a certain trailer park known to house a large percentage of the rival gang who'd made the assault on Gus' property. Not too far from where Pug and I had met and fought the two crackheads on the rusty bridge over the river.

We had acquired four Claymore mines—you know, the kind with "Front Toward Enemy" written on it— and detonators from the stockpiles at the secret ware-house in Del City. We would set these around the trailer park and then detonate them to take out all of those crackheads at once. Like setting off a bug bomb inside a nest of roaches.

We drove to Sand Springs, with Pug behind the wheel, of course. No way was I going to go into this sober. The trailer park was in a small valley surrounded by some bulbous hills... about as much elevation as you'd see in this part of Oklahoma. We parked below the top of one of those hills and dropped to our bellies to crawl close enough for a good look.

Below us sat a ring of trailer homes, about twelve of them in a circle. Front doors all facing out. Like frontier wagons arranged to defend from an attack. In the middle of the circle were a few benches and a grill. No activity outside.

Pug pointed as he snuffed out his cigarette. "I don't know if four is going to cut it. I've never actually seen one of these things detonate before."

"I think they've got a pretty wide spray."

"Yeah, but if we had one for each, we could be sure."

I stared down at the arrangement, pondering. "What if we can get all the people out in the middle there, and detonate the mines then?"

"Too risky. We set off some kind of distraction along the edges, there's no guarantee they'll rush out to the center. I mean, they've all got windows, maybe they just crack their blinds and look."

Good point. I chewed on my lip, brain whirling. All

the variables were too hard to control. "Maybe we get lucky, and the explosion opens up a sinkhole beneath them."

Pug grinned. "Maybe. Or maybe the Flying Spaghetti Monster reaches out with his noodly arm and disables the Claymores as soon as we hit those remote detonators."

"You're right. I got nothing."

"I did say this was a bad idea, you know."

I was almost prepared to admit defeat to Pug and say we should pack up and leave, but then it came to me like a bolt of lightning. "I got it. Maybe getting curious is exactly what we want them to do. You still keep lighter fluid in your trunk?"

"I have a little," Pug said.

"So here's what we do: we set up the four Claymores in the middle, one pointing in each direction. Then, we light a fire somewhere. Maybe in that grill. Not an explosion or anything that would spook everybody and make them run out their front doors, just something to get their attention. Then everyone goes to the inner side of their trailers to look. That's when we hit the Claymores, when they're all close."

Pug rubbed a hand under his chin. "I don't know. We can't be sure how many of them are home, even."

"They're home," I said. "This is a crack den, and it's not even noon yet. Trust me, they're all sleeping."

"I'm starting to come around, I'll admit it. We set

the charges, two remote detonators each. Then we light up the grill, wait a minute, and blow this mother-effer."

"I'm ready," I said, and I began to rise to my feet, but Pug gripped my arm.

"Wait," he said. Look of anguish on his face. "Before we do this, I have to tell you something."

I rolled over onto my side. "What is it?"

"If I tell you this, you can't tell anyone. Not now, not ever."

I didn't like the worry etched into his face. "Of course, Pug. You know I can keep a secret."

He opened his pack of Parliaments, and a shaky hand withdrew a fresh cigarette. "The other day, after we came back from that pedophile's house and Ramón let into me? It wasn't just because he was holding me responsible for the screw-up."

"What do you mean?"

His lip pursed like he was on the verge of tears. He lit the cigarette and took a couple of long drags before replying. "About a week ago, Ramón asked me to come up to his apartment. He had some rare Patrón, he said. Said it was a one-time offer and didn't give me much of a choice."

"Ramón shared his private tequila stock with you?"

"I know, right? I was shocked too, but I couldn't tell him no. So I went up to his apartment, and we had some shots, smoked a couple joints."

He trailed off, staring at the trees on this hilltop, which had started to sway with a light breeze.

"Uh," I said, "I'm assuming there's more to this story, right?"

"He gave me a blowjob."

"Ramón did *what?*"

Pug nodded gravely. "It's true. He was sloppy drunk and stoned like a gargoyle, and he kept pawing at the fly of my jeans. I couldn't say no to that, either."

The reality of the situation started to sink in. "He's married. With kids back in Mexico, even. Is he gay or something?"

"Not that I know of. But he wouldn't be the first straight guy to take a walk on the wild side with me."

"Gross, Pug."

"Oh, so you can tell me every little detail about all the hoochies you bang, but I can't say anything?"

I cleared my throat. "Fair point."

"It's all like some twisted nightmare. Since that night, he's been so cruel to me. He was always a jerk, but not like this. I'm scared, Mike. I don't know what he would do to me if anyone else found out about it. You've heard what they say about gay people when they think there are none around. Wouldn't he rather get rid of me than let this secret out?"

"You can run. Just pack up your stuff and go to Canada or something."

Pug shook his head. "You saw what he did to that kid

who came back to visit his sick mom. Don't you think he'd come after me to keep me from blabbing it or posting this on the internet? I'm pretty sure he'd follow me to the ends of the earth to keep me quiet. Right now, while I'm under his thumb, he probably feels like he can control me. But he might change his mind."

"Pug, there's a way out of this."

He raised an eyebrow. "What way is that?"

"I can't tell you yet. But you have to trust me. We take care of these crackheads, and then everything else is going to get better. This is step one."

"I don't get it."

"Do you trust me?"

"Of course, I trust you," he said.

"Then I have to keep you in the dark a little longer. But it's going to get better."

He pursed his lips and searched my eyes, then eventually, he said, "okay. I believe you."

We helped each other to our feet and retrieved all of the goods we needed from the back of the car. Stacking those Claymores in Pug's backpack made me nervous as hell. The things had to be at least forty years old, maybe even older than that. The remote detonators, though, were high-tech and looked fresh off the assembly line.

Once we were geared up, we started down the hill, but I threw an arm out to stop Pug when I saw some motion down near one of the trailers.

"Raccoon," Pug said.

"They'll have plenty to pick through when we're done," I said, and once the words had left my mouth, I realized how calloused they sounded. How killing people had become almost normal in such a short span of time.

And then I considered all the things I'd done in service of the Sinaloa before this week. I'd broken bones. I'd put people in the hospital. I'd threatened to hurt their children, although, that one, I would never actually do. I'm not a monster, and I don't hurt the innocent. But some shithead drug dealer trying to rip off my employers? Sure, I'd yank out his fingernails with needle-nose pliers. I didn't enjoy doing that, but I sure as hell had done it with gusto.

And now I was going to eviscerate a whole slew of shithead drug dealers. They'd already attacked Gus' place, and if they didn't know where the Freedom House was, they would find out soon. Only a matter of time before they came to kill us all.

Still, what I was about to do here was a terrible thing. I knew that. I could call it self-defense, but that might not last long in the court of my memory.

The bourbon would help, though.

The sky darkened as partly cloudy had turned to mostly cloudy. I worried for a moment about rain, but we'd be done before that could become a problem.

"This ain't our day," Pug said as he ground out his cigarette in the dirt.

"No, it is not. We'll have more after this one."

When we reached the valley, we crept into the middle of the mobile home circle and spread out, with two Claymores each. Pug placed one to the east and one to the north while I covered south and west. We had to hope the spray would be enough to blast apart all twelve of these trailers. Doesn't do any good to shoot a lion with a .22 bullet. You need to tear his face off with a rocket launcher. And if any of these people did survive, we would be perched close by, ready to pick them off as they tried to run.

I handed two of the detonators to Pug, who scurried off to the side. Then, I splashed some lighter fluid onto the grill, squeezing the bottle until it wheezed empty. I found an unopened Dr. Pepper can on the ground and set it on the grill, for good measure. I had no idea if the thing would explode or not, but the twelve-year-old inside of me wanted to see what would happen.

I struck a match from the last book I'd taken home from Willie's Saloon and tossed the little flaming stick onto the grill. The lighter fluid was already catching as I sprinted to meet Pug, crouched behind someone's pickup truck, fifty yards away.

I hustled to meet him and slipped the other two detonators from my pocket. I turned around as the flames were licking the air, and that's when the pop can exploded. Brown liquid foam soared into the air and splatted down like grenade shrapnel. The grill toppled to its side, and the dry grass around it caught fire instantly.

A curtain on one mobile home jerked back and two faces appeared in the window. At the trailer nearest us, the front door opened, and a droopy man wearing only boxer shorts stepped onto his porch.

"Now," I said.

With detonators in each hand, we pressed all four triggers at once.

And nothing happened.

CHAPTER NINETEEN

PUG AND I both frantically clicked the buttons on the detonators, but the Claymores sat motionless, unexploded. The grass around the grill had caught fire, and one of the mines was engulfed in flames, still refusing to explode.

"This is not good," Pug said.

People began filtering out of the mobile homes, and two men came rushing out with fire extinguishers. They stood on opposite sides of the fire and unleashed a torrent of white foam at it.

One man wearing a silky kimono left his trailer, holding a three-foot glass bong in one hand and a lighter in the other. He was bleary-eyed and slack-jawed.

"What do we do?" I said. "If we run, they'll see us."

We were hidden behind the truck, both of our heads poking out around the back of the bed to watch the scene unfold. There was a lot of open space between us and the hilltop where Pug had parked his car.

Pug groaned. "If we don't run, they'll see us eventually anyway. There's nowhere else to hide."

A lanky man with a mohawk paused in front of one of the Claymores and lifted it from the ground. His head cocked, and he stared down at the mine with a confused expression. I watched his eyebrows rise as recognition brightened his face. He looked up and met my eyes. For a split second, neither of us did anything. We were both frozen.

Then, he dropped the mine and pointed at me, screaming. I raised my Beretta at him and squeezed the trigger, but the shot missed wide. My arm had been shaking.

One second later, a half-dozen guns were pointed at me, and the air became a hail of bullets. Most of them pelted the truck Pug and I were hiding behind. Metal tore and cried as holes appeared all over the bed and cab of the truck.

But one bullet came straight for me. I didn't know I'd been hit until my ear felt like it had caught fire. Then, wetness trickled down the side of my face.

I toppled into Pug, who was already returning fire. The gun blasts rattled my brain.

"We need to get out of here," I shouted. "There's too many of them over there. We can't do this."

"You go," Pug said between shots. "I'll follow."

Most of the people in the trailer park had taken cover behind the buildings, popping out to shoot. A few were advancing from cover to cover, inching closer to us with each scramble. I counted fifteen total, all ages, mostly men and only a couple women. No kids, at least. If the mines had worked and I'd found a child's body among the rubble, I don't know if I could have forgiven myself.

Off to the right, one man wearing nothing but tighty-whitey briefs was creeping through the grass, trying to flank us and round the other side of our hiding spot. He was only twenty feet away.

I grabbed Pug's arm and pointed. He lifted his pistol and blasted the man in the stomach. The man spun and fell face-first into the grass, then tried to crawl back toward the trailers.

"Go now," Pug said. "I'll cover you until you're back at the car."

"Hell no," I said. "We go together. Zig-zag up the hill. I'm not going to leave you."

"I told you this was a stupid idea."

"You sure did. Now, let's get out of here so you can remind me later."

I snatched him by the wrist and we ran for the hill.

As my legs churned, blood pumped out of my ear, pulsing warmth down the side of my face.

I could see the nose of Pug's car, parked slightly behind the crest of the hill. Fifty strides to reach it, maybe sixty. But once we started running, we had to stop shooting. Fifteen of them versus zero of us. We'd have to be perfect, and they'd have to be sloppy, or they'd cut us down in a heartbeat.

We crisscrossed each other as we hiked the hill. Shots pelted the angled ground below us. Bits of dirt and rock flew into the air as the crackheads' guns peppered the hillside. When we reached the top, I looked back, and five of them were sprinting up the hill after us.

I took aim at the guy with the mohawk and squeezed the trigger. Hit him square in the chest. He flailed, arms out, and toppled back down the hill. He'd been holding that unexploded Claymore in one hand, and it tumbled alongside him, as harmless as a hunk of cheese.

A bullet whizzed past my hip, and the rush of air made my shorts ripple. For a split second, I felt invincible. Pug and I had taken on a whole damn crackhead army and escaped with almost no ill effect.

"Mike, now!"

Pug had his car keys out, hovering next to his open door. I raced into the passenger seat, and he screeched into reverse, then spun and reconnected with the dirt road that would take us back to a city street.

I looked up into the rearview as two of our assailants crested the hill. One of them raised a rifle, his body spasmed, then a fraction of a second later, the back of Pug's car jerked in response.

"Aw, damn it," Pug said. "Son of a bitch shot my car." He swerved through the neighborhood street as people in houses opened front doors and raised windows to watch us make our hasty getaway.

Would these people take Pug's license plate and call the cops? Probably not. They had to know who their neighbors in the valley were. Redneck neighborhood code of silence.

From a patch of darkened clouds a few miles away, a lightning bolt reached out and stabbed at the ground. Like a scratch across the sky.

I reached up and tapped my wound, grateful to discover that my ear hadn't been blown off. It didn't even feel misshapen. I pointed my injury at Pug. "Is my ear missing a chunk?"

He shook his head. "It's just bleeding a little. Must have only nicked you."

"Hurts like hell. Swear to God I thought that mohawk asshole took it off."

"You'll be fine," Pug said.

He sailed across the intersection at the edge of the neighborhood, flooring it. We still had another mile to the highway. I kept checking the rearview for cars coming after us but didn't see a thing. Maybe they weren't the chasing type. Maybe these crackheads were more calculating than that.

"I think we're good. You can slow down now."

Pug gritted his teeth. "We're pretty far from good."

"So, that didn't go as planned. But all things aside, we made it out alive, and that counts for something."

He frowned, smacked the steering wheel. "Doesn't count for much. Ramón is going to kill us for this."

I think applying the hydrogen peroxide to my ear injury might have hurt worse than getting shot. But, Pug had been right, my ear was all there. A little flap of flesh had been severed, but I bandaged it back in place. With a little luck, it would heal, and no one would be able to tell. I liked to think I wasn't a vain man, but no one wants to walk around with half a missing ear.

Crackhead gang threat not neutralized. Wolf business card not acquired. Things were getting worse, not better.

Standing in the bathroom of my Stillwater apartment, Boba Fett stared at me from his spot in the soap tray. His smug and severed head rested on a bed of dried soap mush.

"What?" I said.

They all saw your face, Boba said. *They're going to come after you. Returning home was not the smartest idea you could have implemented.*

"I'm not sure where that ranks on my current list of problems, but yeah, it's one of them."

What are you going to do about it?

"I am going to go down to Willie's and have a drink. If Krista is there, I'm going to show off my new injury and see if I can convince her I got it saving kittens from a grease fire at an animal shelter."

Good luck with that. You're still not boyfriend material, even with two full ears.

"You can be a real judgmental prick sometimes, Boba."

I stowed him in my pocket and left the apartment, then wandered down the block to Willie's Saloon. She was there, pouring a glass of Guinness for some frat boy. Gave me a wink when I entered, then she nodded at an unoccupied stool at the far end of the bar.

I had a seat, realized for the first time today that my stomach ached from boxing with Pug this morning. And then, a pang of sadness swept over me. Even if I survived long enough to get Witness Protection, and even if I was able to keep Pug out of jail with my testimony, we wouldn't be able to hang out in our new lives. I'd have to go somewhere separate, with a new name. Anonymous and alone.

I would be Carl Terwilliger, an accountant from Detroit, who had moved to Southern California for a fresh start. I'd have played high school football until a knee injury forced me out of the game. Maybe I could have played in college, or, who knows, gone pro. *Oh, do I have any pictures from my high school days or a yearbook I could show you? No, I'm afraid I don't have anything like that. Yeah, it's funny. My past seems to be entirely made up, doesn't it? I promise it's totally legit, though.*

Then, I realized, I could never be an accountant. I had so little real-life work experience that I wasn't qualified to do anything. In this new life in WitSec, I'd be pushed into some data entry job, or they would make me the night custodian at an apartment building, working the graveyard shift so I didn't have to interact with too many people.

I would be like a ghost walking among the normies. An afterthought.

The image unsettled me and I brushed it away. My odds of living through the next four days were slim enough that I didn't need to give those post-Sinaloa considerations any space in my head.

As I sat and waited for Krista to finish flirting with some other guy, I thought about the wolf card I'd failed to extract from Gus. Maybe I could get another crack at it. Not at his house, obviously, but there was a good chance he'd take it around with him. Maybe he would show up at the Freedom House and I could bump into him, then lift his wallet. Snatch the card somehow, without him noticing.

Sure, I'd magically become good at pickpocketing, sometime in the next couple days.

Krista moseyed down to my end of the bar. "Hey, handsome."

"Hey, yourself."

"What happened to your ear?"

"Would you believe me if I told you I was rescuing children from a fire at an orphanage?"

She swished her lips back and forth like she was pretending to consider it. "I can tell you that I would *like* to, but no, I don't think so."

"Then I won't tell you that."

"Okay, then. What can I get you this afternoon?"

"How about a shot of Jack and a Fat Tire in a bottle?"

"You got it." She started to turn away from me and then paused, frowning. "What's going on, Mike? You look like crap."

I tried to fake being affronted, but I probably didn't sell the expression very well. "That's not a nice thing to say."

"Seriously. Something isn't right with you."

"I don't think you'd believe me if I told you."

She leaned over the bar, pushing her sweet breath and her emerald green eyes in my face. "You'd be surprised at the things I'm willing to believe."

"My situation is bad, Krista, real bad. The people I work for…"

I drifted off, wondering how careful I needed to be.

I'd never told her the name of my employers, of course, but she had to know I wasn't in a civilian job. I'd stumbled in here countless times with black eyes and bruised knuckles. She was clever enough to realize that you don't have days like that working at a bank.

She blinked, waiting for me to continue.

"This sounds silly, but I need to get a particular business card. Having one of those is like having a key that can unlock something else really important. One of my employers has one, and I tried to steal it from him, but it didn't work out. Probably made things worse, actually."

"Okay," she said, "is he the only person that has one of these cards?"

"Probably not."

"So why don't you just steal one from somebody else? Someone who is easier to take it from."

"I don't know," I said, and then halted.

Maybe she had a point. Who else could I steal the card from? It was so simple, yet it hadn't even occurred to me before.

"Be right back with your drinks," she said, and then left me alone at my stool.

My mind raced. Of course, Gus didn't have the only wolf card. People at his same level in the organization had one, and occasionally, loyal soldiers received them like medals of bravery. Some guys were given them to accomplish a specific task.

But who else would have one that I could get access to?

I gripped the edge of the bar and smiled. Felt like an idiot for not thinking of this sooner. I knew exactly who I could take the card from.

CHAPTER TWENTY

I DIDN'T KNOW for a fact that Ramón had one of those business cards with the wolf logo, but there was a chance. I'd only seen them carried around by the top guys, but from time to time, lesser soldiers might receive one for special tasks or whatever. I didn't know the exact protocol.

I recalled one specific instance when a guy who wasn't a boss—more like mid-level management—had been given a card so he could travel to Mexico and speak with some higher-ups without being shot on sight. That was exactly the sort of scenario I was hoping to replicate.

And before I could line up the rest of the dominoes to my WitSec deal, I needed to get the card. And I was betting that Ramón would be important enough to own one.

Maybe I'd get lucky in this case. If not, I didn't know what else I could do to gain an audience with El Lobo. Gus and Ramón would not let me in the room with him, and I couldn't walk up to him without approval.

If I had that card, I could do whatever I wanted. A blank check.

As I drove back to Oklahoma City, I formulated my plan. El Lobo was in Dallas tomorrow. I'd get that card and hustle down to the Lone Star state. With that thing in hand, I could walk into a meeting, say I'd come on behalf of the Oklahoma City crew to deliver some kind of message. Didn't matter what. Without Gus and Ramón nearby, I could say whatever I wanted. And then it wouldn't matter if it got back to them because I'd be long gone, sitting in a government safe house somewhere, as long as I got El Lobo speaking and my phone's voice recorder app caught it all.

I could make this work. If Ramón had the card and I could find a way to steal it from him, I could make this work.

I parked at the back of the Freedom House, stared up at the brick building. Lights from the individual apartments pushed out into the night sky. In the basement, the rehab residents would be in the touchy-feely sobriety group right now, so I didn't need to worry about them.

But I could see a light on in Ramón's apartment. I'd

held out hope that he might be gone this evening, and then I'd need only my lock picking kit to gain entry.

As if on cue, a text message appeared on my phone from Ramón, sent to both Pug and me:

> You two idiots went on an unsanctioned
> raid this morning?

I pursed my lips, trying to think of how to respond. Obviously, there would be punishment for our failure in Sand Springs today. Never mind the initiative we'd displayed by taking it into our own hands. Never mind that we had killed a couple of them, and they had killed exactly zero of us. Ramón would only care that it hadn't been his idea.

I could tell him that I was in the lobby downstairs, ready to talk about it. Then, I sneak past him and have full access to his apartment. But, he'd probably ruin that plan by insisting that I meet him at his apartment instead.

I could ignore this text, open the armory in the storage closet, pilfer a grenade, and then toss it down the hall from his apartment. That would get him out, for sure. But, detonating a live grenade in a building less than a mile from the Oklahoma City Capitol wasn't the most low-key option.

I could find someone on the floor and bribe that person to tell Ramón I was injured downstairs, or that

Gus wanted him to meet him in the parking lot, but Ramón would figure that out quickly. And he'd find out who'd made the payoff. Plus, if I did get him to leave, he might keep the card in his wallet like Gus had. Then I would have wasted my one chance to separate him from it.

Shit. Nothing sounded promising. I wiped some sweat from my brow as I had a sip from my flask. The night humidity had turned central Oklahoma into an omnipresent sauna lately.

In the distance, a cop siren faintly sounded.

And then, as I stared up at the tiny balcony jutting from Ramón's bedroom, a moment of divine intervention came. I knew what to do. My hand reached down to the nub of Boba Fett's head in my pocket. I tapped it a few times for luck and then hopped out of my Jeep.

I climbed the outside fire escape so I wouldn't have to risk encountering anyone in the lobby, but that only gave me access to the second floor. The floor where the recovery people lived.

I found myself outside a closed window, but the lights were on inside. I knocked.

A minute later, a woman who looked to be roughly the same age as me appeared in the bedroom. Cigarette in one hand, a blue book with the words *Alcoholics Anonymous* printed on the cover.

She opened the window. "Can I help you?" A split

second later, her eyes widened. "You're one of those top floor people."

I glanced at the cigarette in her hand. "Isn't smoking in the rooms against the rules?"

"You guys smoke a lot worse than that upstairs," she said, a hint of a snarl crossing her face. "We can smell it, you know. We're supposed to say it's none of our business."

"It *is* none of your business. Aren't you supposed to be in the basement for your group right now?"

She shrugged and dragged on her cigarette.

This conversation wasn't going well. Despite her indignant attitude, I still needed something from her, so I had to play nice. "Um, can I come in? I'm just passing through."

She exhaled cigarette smoke out of her nostrils like a dragon, considering. The wait felt endless. "Sure, whatever."

I slipped into the room, landing on the carpet. "I'm sorry about the weed. I rarely smoke the stuff."

Her eyes drifted to the bulge in my pocket where my flask sat. "But you walk around with one of those. What do you think that does to a bunch of people who are trying to get off booze?"

"I have no idea. Makes it harder, I guess?"

She rolled her eyes. "Yeah, it makes it harder. Some of us are sick and trying to get well. You wouldn't blow smoke in the face of a cancer patient."

"I'm not sure what you want from me. I don't even really live here."

Her cigarette butt sizzled as she dropped it into a coffee cup. She crossed her arms and tossed a pointed sigh at me. "It's fine. Like you said, it's none of my business."

And here I'd thought sober people were supposed to be all full of light and harmony. This chick was nothing but a cauldron of tension and anger, ready to bubble over. Maybe the post-booze life was exactly the drag I'd imagined.

I didn't know what to say to her, so I left her with a half-hearted smile and dashed out of the apartment. Hit the stairs and rushed up to the top floor, where I eased open the door a smidgen to ensure that Ramón wasn't hanging out in the hallway.

His door was shut, so I slinked past it. Mexican music warbled from behind his closed door. My phone buzzed. Checked a new message, and Pug had responded to Ramón's group text:

I can explain.

I thought about typing something but resisted the urge. Soon, none of this would be a problem anymore, if I could only get that damn card.

At the next door, I smacked the flat of my palm

against it, careful not to be too loud. A minute later, the door opened. "Michael?"

Standing on the other side of the door was Tanner, the same kid from the warehouse who had brought in that unlucky escape artist. Frowning at me. I'd never really looked at Tanner up close before. Couldn't have been more than sixteen years old. A minor. That gave me some comfort, to know that he probably wouldn't see any jail time after Delfino flipped the switch and everyone went away in handcuffs.

"Hey, Tanner. Can I come in?"

"Sure, dude. Something going on?"

I slid inside his apartment and shut the door behind me. "Nope. Nothing's going on. This is going to sound strange, but I need to get on your balcony for a second."

"Huh?"

"It's better if you don't ask any questions."

His head tilted to the left, and his eyes narrowed. A pulse of fear boiled my stomach. I'd assumed Tanner would do whatever I said without hesitation, but his expression suggested he wasn't buying it.

"I don't know," he said. "This is kinda weird. Maybe I should go ask Ramón."

I had a split second notion of grabbing him and putting him in a sleeper hold. But, if I didn't accidentally choke him to death, doing that was something I couldn't come back from. People would find out about it. If Tanner were willing to snitch on the kid with the sick mother, he would certainly do the same to me.

Tanner took a step to walk past me, but I backed up against his door. "No. Hear me out."

He crossed his arms in front of his chest. Waited for me to speak.

"What I'm going to tell you is totally confidential."

He raised an eyebrow. "Alright."

"Gus sent me. Ramón is on the outs, and I need to get into his apartment. But I can't go in the front because he can't know about it. So, in a second, the cops are going to be here. Whatever you do, stay in your apartment, and don't come out. You'll be fine."

"This is what Gustavo wants?"

I nodded.

"Alright, dude. Whatever you need."

After a quick word of thanks and another request that he keep this our secret, I left Tanner in the living room and exited to his balcony from the bedroom. Ramón's balcony was only three feet away, so I wasn't going to have to pull any kind of Jason Bourne action stunt to get there. I slipped across, keeping my body hidden from Ramón's bedroom window. Didn't hear any music coming from the apartment anymore.

I leaned forward, peering inside. Ramón had his back to me, hunched over on his bed. Across from him, on his nightstand, sat an open laptop. A gay porn video playing on the screen. Two naked men grunting against each other.

Then, I noticed Ramón's arm moving.

If I ever wanted to get rid of Ramón, all I'd have to do would be to snap a picture of this moment and then email it out to everyone. But, I didn't want him executed by Gus for spanking it to videos of men having sex. I wanted him behind bars with the rest, away from Pug and me.

And to do that, I needed his damn wolf card. If he even had one, which I was about to find out, one way or the other.

I slipped out my phone and dialed.

"911. What's your emergency?"

"Yes," I said, keeping my voice low. "I'm staying at the Freedom House on Culbertson. There are some houses on the other side of the street. Like those duplexes, you know? Someone is shooting off a gun over there. I heard a woman screaming."

"Sir, can you tell me—"

"The shooting is still going on. Please send someone."

I hung up. Waited three minutes, and then looked back inside. Ramón wasn't jerking off anymore. He was now sitting at the desk across from his bed, rolling a joint over a wooden tray.

Sirens echoed from down the street. Ramón angled

his head, listening. Then, he jumped up, closed his robe, and darted out of the bedroom.

I waited another thirty seconds and opened the sliding glass door on his balcony. Assumed I'd have maybe one full minute until he figured out that the sirens were across the street and therefore nothing to be concerned about.

I went straight for his pants and snatched his wallet. Thumbed through his credit cards and cash. No wolf card.

I yanked open the nightstand to the left of his bed. Found two weed pipes, a bottle of lube, and a pile of used Breathe Right nasal strips. But no card.

I raced around to the other nightstand and jerked it open. There, sitting among stacks of rolled-up twenty dollar bills: a single white business card with a raised image of a wolf's head. Slight watermark, barely visible, that read *Lobo*.

Jackpot.

CHAPTER TWENTY-ONE

I PARKED ALONG Kelley Avenue and reclined my seat, Ramón's wolf card burning in my pocket like one of those chemical hand warmers. Some people I knew would say that sitting in a parked car on Kelley was a poor decision for a white boy, but I'd never cared about that noise. Besides, I had a Beretta in my glove box, and I'd already shot three people in the last week.

I slept a couple hours in my Jeep before heading south to Dallas. The drive would take about three hours, since I was technically going to Plano, and not Dallas proper.

Plano was a northern suburb full of rich people like retired Dallas Cowboys players and tech startup entrepreneurs who'd cashed out at age thirty. The land of wide highways, mega-malls and mega-churches, chain restaurants and parking lots that were so spacious they almost required shuttles to get from one end to the other.

I knew almost nothing about the branch of the Sinaloa here other than the address of the apartment complex that served as the headquarters of the operation. It wasn't a covert rehab halfway house like in Oklahoma City. Just a privately owned building on Northwood Lane named Terrace Gardens. Such a peaceful name. A garden on a terrace, maybe with one of those little Zen meditation sandboxes with the rake. I'm sure the reality wasn't anything like that.

As the sun rose to my left, I became keenly aware that I had only three days left until Lobo's scheduled visit to Oklahoma City. If I succeeded here today, that wouldn't matter.

I exited Highway 75 at a little past eight in the morning. Grabbed some drive-through McDonalds to calm my growling stomach, and then I headed for Terrace Gardens.

I still hadn't worked out exactly what I was going to say when I walked in there. The important thing was that I turn on the voice recorder app on my phone beforehand. Then, as long as Velasquez said anything to do with him or his business, I'd have all I needed. Wouldn't even have to worry about the rest of the chain of events. I'd strut into the FBI field office in Stillwater, hold up my phone and say, *"see, you smug bitch? I told you I could do this."*

I parked at an auto parts store across the street from the apartments. Studied the building complex. There were three buildings shaped like a U, with a courtyard out in front. Swing set, play area, park benches. Behind that stood the double doors of the main entrance to the middle building, which would lead me into the lobby.

If I walked in there and slapped my newly-acquired wolf card down on the table at the front desk, someone would point me to him. They had to.

Maybe I could tell him that I suspected Ramón of doing something shady, and offer to kill him. Then I get El Lobo ordering the hit on tape so I have my evidence, and I go straight to meet Special Agent Delfino. I kept picturing the shock on her face when she would realize that I'd come up with a better plan than she had.

But, if I was going to throw around accusations about Ramón, I needed more than words. Now I wished I had actually snapped that picture of Ramón whacking off to gay porn. These people treated homosexuality as a crime, and that would have been all the evidence I'd have needed to convict Ramón.

But a scary thought occurred to me: what if Gus were here, in Plano? I hadn't seen or heard from him since breaking into his house two days ago. If I ran into him here, all bets were off.

Maybe strutting across to Terrace Gardens wasn't

going to be as easy as I'd thought. Maybe I needed to take inventory of the people at the complex first.

Somewhere, lost in all this thought, I must have drifted off, because the next thing I knew, I was opening my eyes to the sound of a car horn honking. Some pedestrian spending too long to cross at the intersection.

The world phased in around me, and I had to take a moment to remember where I was and why I was here. I checked my phone. Had been asleep for an hour in the driver's seat. I turned my head from side to side to pop my neck and stretch my back. If I didn't get a good night's sleep soon, I was going to collapse.

I squinted across the street at the apartments, and my jaw dropped. There he was; Luis Velasquez, AKA El Lobo. I knew him from the bushy beard and the barrel chest. Seeing him in person sent a jagged knife of panic into my chest. How could I approach this man and talk to him, knowing that the full weight of the federal government was prepared to come down on him? And, that I was the one helping to aim the hammer?

I felt fairly confident that if I stood within ten feet of him, he'd smell the deceit on me in an instant. He'd have someone knock me out with a baseball bat. I'd wake up in a meat locker, hanging from one of those hooks they use to suspend slabs of dead cow. Then, a group of my peers would torture me until I'd told them everything, and I would beg them for death.

My palms dampened. The Egg McMuffin in my belly swirled.

And then I noticed the strangest thing. El Lobo wasn't alone out there in the courtyard. He lifted a little girl up onto the swing set and stood behind her, pushing her on that swing. She was laughing, and he started laughing too. She looked just like him, except without the beard and the middle-aged girth, of course.

His daughter. Had to be.

Velasquez had always been legendary for his cruelty. I'd heard stories of him executing hundreds of people, including a dozen of his own captains once because they'd failed to successfully bribe some government official in Juarez. The stories painted him as a blood-drenched warrior, second only to Vlad the Impaler.

And here he was, giggling along with his daughter while he pushed her on the swing. *Higher daddy, push me higher.*

Now, said Boba Fett from my pocket. *Forget all of your fears and do it. Do this now while you still have time.*

I opened the door to my Jeep and stumbled out, just as a car pulled up behind me, blocking me in. Tires screeched to a halt and the sudden sound threw me off balance. I tripped and landed in the parking lot.

When I looked up, Pug pivoted in the driver's seat, glaring at me.

My eyes unfocused as Pug stepped out of his car. I

staggered to my feet, desperately on the verge of puking. "Pug?"

"Mike. What the hell are you doing here?"

I careened toward him. "How did you find me? How did you know to come here?"

He held up his phone. "You shared your location with me on the Find My Friends app, remember? I had a feeling you were going to disappear on me again like I asked you *not* to do, and you went and did it anyway."

I blinked. Had a vague memory of us both downloading the same GPS app a few months ago, but I didn't remember linking them together. Must have been drunk at the time.

Pug frowned. "I'm glad I remembered I had this app yesterday, or I wouldn't have been able to watch your little avatar drive all the way down here in the middle of the night."

"Okay, so, I'm in Plano," I said. "I know why I'm here, but what are you doing here?"

He nodded across the street. "I'm here to keep you from doing something stupid; something you'll regret for the rest of your short life."

"What do you think I'm going to do?"

He pointed across the street. "I know it looks like he's alone out there with that little kid, but I can see at least three men aiming sniper rifles up on the roof. And four more sitting in cars in the parking lot with loaded machine guns."

"So?"

"You won't make it halfway across the courtyard."

"You think I'm here to kill Velasquez?"

His head jerked to the side. "You're not?"

I shook my head, still a little stunned that Pug was standing in front of me. Really here. So much had happened in the last few seconds, I could barely breathe. My head was racing too fast to make sense of it all.

He snatched me by the arm and pulled me away from my car. I followed him around to the back of the auto parts store, and we sat next to a pile of tires.

"Even if I was going to kill him," I said. "I still don't get why you raced down here after me."

He rubbed his hands together and took a few measured breaths. "I have to tell you something. I haven't been honest with you. They told me if I breathed a word of it to anyone that it would ruin everything, but I can't keep this from you. Not any longer. Not if you're going to be running around, doing stupid shit like this."

"Pug, you need to start making sense."

His mouth opened for a second, suspended in air. He took a cigarette from behind his ear and stuck it between his lips. "The feds approached me. They've offered me Witness Protection."

I gasped. "They did *what?*"

"I was getting a massage at that little place in Brick-town, the one I like with the jazz music. They came right in during the middle of my session, kicked the masseuse out, and laid it out there in front of me. My family's land? They're going to buy it for me, Mike. I'll get the deed, free and clear."

"How is that Witness Protection if you're still living in Oklahoma?"

"I won't live on the land, but that's fine. But I'll finally own it, and I can have someone else dredge the whole thing to find that hidden stash."

"And then what happens to me?" I said.

He shook his head slowly, mournfully. "They said you'd probably get charged with drug trafficking, but if I played along, they could work with the prosecutors to ease the charges. You'd do two years, maybe three. But only if this goes well, and I wasn't supposed to tell you."

"They're a bunch of liars, Pug. Don't trust a word they say."

His lips pursed. "What do you mean?"

"They offered me WitSec too."

Pug didn't have a response for this. He sat back and examined his fingernails for a few seconds. Puffed his cigarette. "Then why are you here, trying to kill El Lobo?"

"Damnit, Pug, listen to me. I'm not trying to kill him. I'm trying to get him on tape, admitting to something."

"That's never going to work. He'll spot you coming before you get onto the building's lawn, and then have his sharpshooters take off your head with a flick of his wrist."

I hadn't wanted to see it, but he was absolutely right. Coming here had been a stupid idea. I couldn't just walk up to the man, unannounced, even with the wolf card. I needed to have Gus' or Ramón's blessing. Lobo would require a warning about the arrival of someone he didn't know. Why would he react in any other way than shooting first?

"You're right. I didn't think this through all the way because I'm an idiot."

"That shouldn't surprise you," he said, with a hint of a smile.

I didn't much feel like smiling back. "I'm so tired. Feel like I haven't slept in weeks."

He nodded, staring at the ground.

"What do we do now?"

"We go home," he said as he dug a hand into his pocket and pulled out two flash drives.

"What's that?"

"I've been meaning to give you these. One is that music collection I've promised you forever. The other one is a little harder to explain. I don't feel like I should hold onto it anymore."

"I'm not following."

He sighed. "I downloaded some spreadsheets from Gus' computer a few months ago. It was risky and stupid of me, but I have it now, and I don't know what to do with it."

"Spreadsheets of what?"

"No idea. I don't know what they mean, or if they mean anything at all. But you should have them."

"Why?"

He held them out to me and shook his head. "Just take them, please."

Pug dropped the two flash drives into my hand, and I rolled them around in the flat of my palm. Two little pieces of plastic, clicking together. He clapped me on the shoulder, and I closed my hand around them. Shoved the drives into my pocket.

"Let's go home," he said.

I blinked a few times and accepted that he was right. I couldn't make any progress here today. Felt like a failure.

With that, we both stood up and returned to our cars so we could drive back home together. Failures, but still alive, at least.

CHAPTER TWENTY-TWO

I SAT OUTSIDE the FBI field office in Stillwater on Western Road, fuming. My jaw ached from grinding my teeth for hours. I'd raced back here so I could intercept Delfino by lunchtime, fueled by rage and a sense of justice.

My hands squeezed the steering wheel with such force I worried I might rip it from the steering column. That would have been better than what I actually wanted to do. I literally had to tell myself, more than once, not to pull my Beretta from the glove box and shoot up the building.

I wondered if the FBI had any intention of keeping their word to either me or Pug. If that proposed Witness Protection deal Delfino had dropped on my floor the other day had been all forgery. Or, if maybe they'd planned to play Pug and me against each other.

Put us in separate rooms, claim the other one was willing to give up better information, and that only one of us would leave with the get-out-of-jail-free card.

These people didn't know Pug or me. They looked at us and saw criminals who would sell out their own mothers. They didn't think we were anything more than pieces of meat to be thrown to the dogs to fill their bellies. Tools to be used and thrown away.

Well, to hell with that. I was not going to keep my mouth shut and let them get away with this.

At around noon, the front door opened, and Delfino exited the building with a tall white man. Both of them with mirrored sunglasses. They were chatting, headed for the parking lot.

I hopped out of my Jeep and stomped across the yard to intercept them. "You conniving bitch," I said, nearly screaming.

The man with Delfino slid a hand into his suit coat, but Delfino stopped him with a finger. "Michael," she said, wearing a plastic smile. "You really shouldn't be here."

"Did you think I wouldn't find out? This lunkhead with you, is he the one handling Pug? Are you comparing notes on the expendable chess pieces you're moving around the board?"

She held out her hands with her palms down, pressing them toward the ground. "Okay, okay, let's keep it down. If you want to talk, we can go inside.

Please do not make a scene out here." She whispered something to the guy she was with, and he left us, his eyes scoping me until he'd disappeared into the parking lot.

She approached me cautiously, clasping her hands in front of her waist. "Let me explain."

"A piece of the puzzle, you said. I thought it was weird at the time, but I shrugged it off. Now, it makes total sense. Pug's my backup, isn't he? The failsafe plan in case things don't work out?"

She removed her sunglasses, fire in her eyes. "Is that what you think? No, Michael, *you* are the backup plan. Do you think we'd pin all our hopes on a drunk and screw up like you? You can barely walk a straight line most of the time. Why would we put all of our eggs in your basket? Why would we entrust this investigation— which has been three years in the making—into your shaky hands?"

My voice caught in my throat. I stammered, trying to get some kind of argument out, but couldn't find the words. I wanted to disagree with her assessment of me, but I couldn't even do that.

"That's what I thought," she said. "Yes, Michael McBriar, you are expendable. You're not a social worker who volunteers at an animal shelter on the weekends. You are a foot soldier who works for a Mexican drug cartel. You're not even a good foot soldier."

"Okay," I said, feeling about ten inches tall.

"Don't think for a second that you get to dictate terms. Our relationship is not negotiable."

I realized that I couldn't trust them to keep their word about WitSec for Pug or for me, but I could definitely trust them to keep their word about putting me in prison.

For a few beats, we both stood in silence.

All that fire I'd had burning inside me a few minutes ago had withered to flickering embers. I didn't actually want to rot in prison for the rest of my life. I wanted my freedom. I wanted a fresh start.

I didn't see that I had any other choice than to comply.

"I get it," I said. "But I can still do this."

"We're not even sure if Velasquez is keeping his meeting three days from now. If you want a chance to be a part of this, find that out. We haven't been able to learn if he's changed his itinerary. Can you do that?"

"I'm going to prove you wrong."

She slipped on her sunglasses and sighed. "I sure hope so, for your sake. Otherwise, get used to the idea of wearing khaki and denim every day, just like the rest of them will."

CHAPTER TWENTY-THREE

AFTER A TEXT had ordered me back to Oklahoma City, I sped along the highway, my thoughts racing faster than my car. Forget Delfino and her threats, I couldn't stop puzzling over why Pug had given me those flash drives back in Plano. The look on his face. The way he'd been dismissive about it.

He'd been promising me that flash drive full of music for months. Why give it to me now? And why would I care about some spreadsheets full of whatever?

The not knowing sizzled my insides.

When I pulled up to Freedom House, Ramón was standing out front, arms crossed, a scowl on his face. He made a big show of checking his watch.

"This is why I don't like you living in Stillwater," he

said as he hopped in my Jeep. "When I text you, I want you here in ten minutes."

"If this is about what happened in Sand Springs yesterday—"

"Oh, don't you worry. We're gonna talk about that. Gus is coming here later, and we're going to talk to both of you about that, believe me. But now, Mr. Driver, you drive."

A thought popped into my brain: *kill Ramón. Take him out now. He's too unpredictable. He's going to get in the way.*

I had a knife in my pocket. Just a little switchblade—nothing special—but it would be good enough to slit Ramón's throat right now. Kill him and dump his body in a ditch somewhere out in the boonies.

Killing Ramón was obviously a bad idea, but still tempting. I could eliminate the possibility that he might fire me and ban me from the Sinaloa for the botched raid on the trailer park.

"What are you waiting for? Drive."

I exited the parking lot with no idea where I was supposed to go. Ramón's knees bounced, his heels stomping against the floor of my car. He slipped a little glass container from his shirt pocket and pressed it under his nose. Jerked his head back, bits of white powder floating out into the air.

So, today was a coke day, not a weed day. Or maybe

the weed would come later. I knew not to test him on a day like this.

He pointed to my left.

"The highway?" I said.

He nodded and snorted again from the glass bullet.

"It would help if I knew where we were going," I said.

"South."

"Okay, we go south."

I joined I-35, thinking maybe we were headed for Norman or Moore. Maybe he'd tell me where to exit the highway, or maybe he'd yell at me for not telepathically knowing which exit I was supposed to take.

We rode in silence for a few minutes as he continued to fidget in his seat. I kept looking at objects near the side of the highway I could use as an excuse to create an accident. Ramón wasn't wearing his seatbelt. I could drift and crash the car into the median. If I were going above thirty, he'd fly right through the windshield. I might only get a few bumps and bruises. Just a slip of the steering wheel, maybe a fake sneeze, in case he somehow survived and I had to make an excuse later.

But I knew I couldn't do that. The feds would figure out I'd killed Ramón, and they'd nullify my deal. And by extension, Pug's chance at freedom. I had to see this through.

And thinking of the deal, I remembered that I was still on the hook to find out if Velasquez was going to keep his visit. Since I'd blown my chance in Plano, I needed this to happen.

I decided to prod a little. "Where we're going, does this have something to do with El Lobo's visit?"

He sneered at me. "What do you know about it?"

"Nothing, nothing. I just heard he was coming in a couple days."

"Yes, well. It has nothing to do with you."

I pressed my lips together. It wasn't exactly an iron-clad confirmation, but at least that gave me some hope that Lobo was still planning to be here.

"Do we need to do anything special before he gets here?" I said. "Clean up the building or anything like that?"

He eyed me. "Stop talking about it. You are really getting on my nerves."

"Okay, okay. Sorry."

And I also knew that trying to persuade Ramón to grant me access to the room with El Lobo was pointless. I'd have to work on Gus to make that happen.

Despite all that, I still had a chance. If I could keep Ramón in the dark for long enough, I could burn this whole thing to the ground later.

I sat in the gazebo behind Gus' house, sweating under the oppression of this muggy July evening. I was exhausted. Had spent my morning driving to Plano and back, then my afternoon driving Ramón all over southern Oklahoma City and then here. What I'd really wanted to do was discuss the Delfino conversation with Pug so we could compare notes. Formulate a united front so we could both get Witness Protection.

I leaned forward and put my eighty-pound head in my hands. Needed sleep. It had been days since I'd gotten more than a cat nap. I could have curled up into a ball next to the chair right then.

But Ramón had told me to wait for him out here, so that's what I was doing.

Two of Gus' bodyguards were standing at the edges of the gazebo, stone-faced, mute. Submachine guns cradled in their hands. Otherwise, we were alone, waiting for something to happen.

Pug exited the back of the house, his face down as he crossed the yard and joined me at the gazebo. He closed his eyes as he sat in the chair next to me. Both of us facing the back of the house, waiting for Ramón and Gus.

They were going to yell and scream and berate us for botching the raid in Sand Springs yesterday. And we would have to sit there and take it. Then, we'd go back to work.

"What do we say?" I whispered to Pug.

"Let me do the talking," he whispered back.

The back door opened, and Gus and Ramón appeared in the yard. I tried to get Pug's attention again, and he only shook his head at me.

Gus seemed even and level, as per usual. Ramón was scowling, and I could see how bloodshot his eyes were before he was even a hundred feet away. They entered the gazebo and faced us. Gus across from me, Ramón across from Pug.

"We have to talk about something serious," Gus said.

"Wait," I said. "I can explain."

Gus held up a finger to silence me. "We are a family. That is supposed to mean more than anything. Without family, we are nothing."

"It's my fault," I said. "Making a raid on the trailer park in Sand Springs was my idea. I didn't check the Claymores before we left, and the whole thing turned into a shit-show because of me."

"Enough," Gus said. "We are not here to talk about that."

This caught me off guard. I didn't know what to say. Ramón had promised me retribution for messing up Sand Springs. I tried to catch Pug's expression out of the corner of my eye, but his head was down, mute and still.

"I don't understand," I said.

"You don't understand," Ramón said. "But you will."

Gus cleared his throat. "What happened in the trailer park should not have happened, that's true. There has not been proper communication about taking initiative and what marks the boundary of unacceptable. Because of that, Ramón and I discussed it before we came out and we have decided that it was an understandable mistake."

Then why were we here?

A flash of realization hit me. They knew. They knew about the feds, the Witness Protection offers. That had to be why both Pug and I were here. Or, Gus had gotten around to watching the security tapes from the night I'd broken into his house and had seen me slinking across his yard. He would have assumed Pug was in on it too. They would grill us until we admitted that we were actually working for the Sand Springs gang as spies.

"We have a thief among us," Gus said.

Or, it was something completely different.

Gus opened his wallet and removed his wolf card, and then I understood. The card I'd stolen from Ramón was sitting in my back pocket, burning a hole in my jeans.

"These are sacred," Gus said. "El Lobo himself gives these out to those who are worthy. To possess one of these when you haven't been given it is an offense punishable by death." Then, he knelt down in front of me, looking up into my eyes. "I spoke with Tanner this morning. He said you were behaving strangely in his apartment last night. What were you doing in his apartment, Michael?"

I didn't know what to say, but I knew I had to start speaking immediately. "I was playing a trick on him. It's something a few of the guys do from time to time. It's like an initiation to see if they choose loyalty among us or loyalty to the people we work for. Since he came to talk to you, I can see that he passed."

Gus chewed on his lip for a moment. Ramón, however, didn't seem to be buying it at all. He shifted his weight back and forth from one foot to the other, his teeth gritted and his hands constantly flexing and unflexing at his sides.

"I see," Gus said as he stood up. "We are going to talk with everyone, but your strange behavior had put you at the top of the list. If we do not find out who stole this card—"

"It was me," Pug said.

I jerked my head toward Pug, baffled.

"You?" Ramón said. He almost seemed pleased about Pug's false confession. "I should have known."

Why would Pug take the blame for something like that? Why would he make such a stupid claim?

I couldn't let Pug do this. Nurturing his over-developed sense of loyalty was a poor move right now. If we would both keep our mouths shut, they wouldn't be able to prove a thing.

I opened my mouth to explain that Pug was

mistaken, but before I could, Ramón pulled a Colt .45 from his back pocket.

"Wait!" I said.

Ramón lifted the barrel to Pug's head and squeezed the trigger.

Everything after that happened in slow motion.

Pug's head snapped back and then forward as a spray of red blew out of the back of his head, coating the top of his chair and the frame of the white gazebo in burgundy dots. The two bodyguards wiped blood spatter from their faces.

Pug's body slumped from the chair, folding into a pile at Ramón's feet. His foot jiggled like he was trying to break a case of restless leg syndrome.

I heaved a breath, my ears ringing. Couldn't hear myself yell, but I pushed air from my lungs until I collapsed from the chair, onto my knees. My throat burned.

A puddle of red was spreading out from underneath Pug's head. I could see into his skull. Literally inside his head. See the broken bits of bone and gray brain matter inside the hollowed-out cavity.

My shaking hand reached out and touched his shoulder. He was still warm. His eyes were open, focused on Gustavo's feet.

I had a clear and persistent thought that maybe I could still save him. Maybe I could take the brain and bone and force them back into his skull cavity. If I could get him to the hospital quickly enough, I could save him. Maybe there was still time. I had to do everything I could to save my friend. If I had a chance to save him, didn't I have to take it? Otherwise, what else was I doing all of this for if we weren't both going to survive together?

He couldn't be dead. It wasn't possible.

In another second, I realized that both Gus and Ramón were still speaking to me. Their mouths moved in the shape of words, but I heard only the whine of my ears, residual ringing from the closeness of the gun blast.

Darkness settled over me like a sudden eclipse. I couldn't save Pug. He had a hole in the back of his head I could have put my fist through. His brains were scattered in a ten foot arc from his body, dotting the white wooden floor of Gustavo Salazar's gazebo.

Ramón had squeezed the trigger. I had seen it happen.

Ramón jabbed me on the shoulder with his pistol. "You listening? Going to cry a river over this fucking *maricón*?"

"Enough," Gus said. "As far as I'm concerned, we can consider this matter closed. If the card turns up, then maybe we worry about it later."

Ramón leaned down, an inch from my face. "If I find out this was actually you, I'm not going to kill you so quickly. You understand?"

I couldn't answer. I was looking through Ramón, to the clear sky behind him. Trying to figure out if this was really happening. Dimly, I recalled that I had driven Ramón here. I would have to drive him back to the Freedom House after this. I would have to share a car with the man who had murdered my best friend, and I couldn't do anything about it.

This couldn't be happening.

Was this really happening?

Ramón grabbed the collar of my shirt and jerked me to my feet, then pulled our faces so close together that our noses touched. My eyes unfocused, and the world swam around me. Ramón's eyes were orbs of fire, his lips hiding rings of jagged and yellowed fangs.

"DO YOU UNDERSTAND ME?"

CHAPTER TWENTY-FOUR

I WOKE UP in the afternoon, sprawled face-first in my Papasan chair. Shoulders aching. My head was wrenched to the side, craning my neck at a horribly weird angle. I pulled my head back an inch and a line of spit connected my lips to the chair's cushion. My mouth felt like I'd been sucking on a wad of dryer lint.

I reached a hand to my back and felt something perched there. Grasped it, and turned in the chair to find myself holding a bag of some foul-smelling dirt weed. The kind of stuff dealers sell to stupid college kids who don't know any better. *Oh yeah, man, this is totally hydroponic, straight from Brazil. Good shit.*

And I also now noticed many new places on my body that hurt. A half dozen or maybe more. The side of my face ached, and so did my hands. I spun to sit in the chair properly and noticed dried blood in my knuckle grooves. At least I didn't have a pair of sawed-through handcuffs dangling from one wrist. That was a positive, at least.

My memories of last night were like a chalkboard wiped to a blurry clean. Couldn't recall how I'd gotten home, where I'd been drinking, how the hell I'd gotten this bag of weed.

I groaned to rise to my feet and found that both of my knees were so sore I could barely stand. Stumbled into the bathroom and learned that I'd somehow generated a welt on the side of my face so big it was like having a third cheek.

What the hell happened to me last night?

Like a series of camera flash bursts, some of it came back. My best friend was dead. I'd seen his brains scattered all over the inside of a gazebo in Oklahoma City last night. Ramón, my boss, had placed the barrel of a gun against his head and squeezed the trigger. I remembered the deafening roar of the gun, only a couple feet from my ears.

And then I'd driven home, and then… the rest was a blur.

I didn't know what had happened between then and now, but I knew exactly how I ended up here. In the grander interpretation of the phrase. I was a screw up, plain and simple. I'd screwed up college by flunking out. I'd been unable to keep a job after college. I'd been too cowardly to leave the Sinaloa, even though I knew how terrible they were. Instead, I drank myself into oblivion anytime I began to feel terrible about the terrible things I was doing as a soldier in their service.

And Delfino was right... I wasn't even a good cartel soldier. I kept my head down and did my work, but I was always on the verge of getting in trouble. Always almost too drunk to get the job done.

I had a brother and a sister and two parents who wanted nothing to do with me, and for good reason. I could be dead, for all they cared. And I deserved it. I had hurt each and every one of them enough times that they had no reason to continue to give me chances.

I had no prospects, no hope, no reason to do anything but drink myself to death. A grim image of a funeral played in my head. No one came forward to give a eulogy.

And now that Pug had died, I had no friends. Ramón had stolen my only friend away from me. Had erased the only person who'd truly known me and had accepted me for the pathetic screw-up I was.

I leaned forward and puked into the sink. Couldn't tell what I'd eaten from the contents. Took another look at my bruised knuckles and concentrated, trying to piece the events together. Nothing materialized other than a few brief glimpses: glasses clinking, lights flashing. Buying a drink for some guy with a beard so long it was braided like a young girl's hair. I had a split second memory of me standing outside the Stonewall Tavern down the street, trying to piss against the side of the building, then falling flat on my face on the sidewalk. And then maybe something about jumping into Theta Pond on campus? Too murky to know for sure.

If I'd gotten the bloody knuckles by hitting a person, that might explain the welt on my cheek. For all I knew, as soon as I stepped out into the walkway outside my apartment, I was going to encounter a whole slew of angry fraternity brothers. Maybe I had hit on someone's girlfriend.

On the floor in the bathroom sat an unopened pack of Parliament cigarettes. Pug's brand. I rarely smoked, and hated the way the stink clung to my clothes and my hair. I must have gone out last night to buy these. With a grunt, I leaned down and opened the pack, and then took out two cigarettes and flipped them over, then reinserted them back into the pack upside down. The last two lucky cigarettes. A ritual Pug used to do with every pack he'd ever bought, for as long as I'd known him.

"You can scratch cancer off the list, Pug," I said as I tossed the pack into the trash can.

Hearing his name come out of my own mouth was like a dagger in the chest. I didn't want to say his name. Didn't want to hear anyone else say his name either, ever again. Saying his name made it real, and I didn't know if I'd ever be able to handle that.

I picked Boba Fett out of my pocket and dropped him in the soap tray.

"That's it, Boba. I'm done. I don't give a shit anymore. Not about Witness Protection, or El Lobo, or that stupid Sand Springs gang, or any of it."

Don't do that, Boba said. *There's still a chance. You have two more days to figure out how to get El Lobo on tape. To have a chance at a future. Listen to me: there's still time.*

I retched again, my abs aching as I expelled my stomach. "Forget about time. I could have all the time in the world, and it wouldn't matter."

Do it for Pug.

"Do what for him? He's dead."

You know what I mean.

I looked up at my garish reflection in the mirror, and I understood what Boba was saying.

Ramón.

I had to kill that fucker.

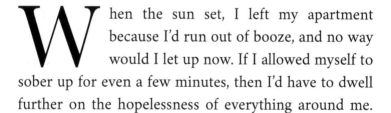

When the sun set, I left my apartment because I'd run out of booze, and no way would I let up now. If I allowed myself to sober up for even a few minutes, then I'd have to dwell further on the hopelessness of everything around me. And I wasn't interested in letting that happen.

As my shoe thudded onto the wooden walkway

outside my apartment, my phone rang. Blocked number.

"Hello?"

"It's Tanner."

My lips curled into a grimace. "You little bastard. You couldn't do me one favor and keep your mouth shut—"

"Wait. Hear me out. I know about Pug. I had no idea Ramón was going to freak out like that, and I'm so, so sorry. If I knew what I'd told him would result in him shooting Pug... you have to believe me, Mike."

I said nothing.

Tanner cleared his throat. "I want to make it up to you."

I had to unclench my jaw to speak. "Start talking."

"Are you at home right now?"

"Yeah. What about it?"

"You need to get out of there."

"What are you saying? What do you know that I don't?"

"Gus and Ramón are using you as bait to draw out that Tulsa gang. They told them your address, and that it was you that attacked the trailer park in Sand Springs. If it works, they should all be on their way to you right now, and we're supposed to pick them off in town. There's a dozen of us here in Stillwater, scattered around."

"I'm bait?"

"Listen to me, Mike. Get the hell out of there. Don't let yourself be cornered. Go to a bar or the library or even hide out at the police station. Just don't be at home when—"

I ended the call and ducked back into my apartment to grab my Beretta. I could barely stand up straight, but if those Sand Springs crackheads were coming, I was going to be ready for them.

I caught a flash of white on my kitchen counter. The wolf business card, sitting between a cluster of empty beer bottles. If I had never taken that card, Pug would still be alive. I'd set all of these events into motion.

Pug's death was my fault.

A car horn honked outside, and I came to my senses. I had to get out now. I rushed out the front door and down the wooden steps to the gravel parking lot, and I saw three people I recognized from the Freedom House at the edge of my parking lot. They nodded at me.

I ignored them and jogged down the block to Washington. The sidewalks and street were thick with college kids.

Wasn't it summertime? Why were there so many people in town?

"Hey," I said to some girl in a sundress and a cap with giant alien antennae on it. "What's going on?"

"It's Joe's weekend, home slice," she said. "You been hiding in a cave or something?"

Joe's weekend. Stillwater's flagship bar and restaurant, Eskimo Joe's. The bar's anniversary weekend, when the whole town turned into one big street party. Gus and Ramón had lured the crackhead gang here? Did it have to be today, when there were a thousand people out in the streets in Stillwater?

Gus and Ramón had done this on purpose, of course. If shots rang out in a crowd, the pandemonium would give our guys a better chance at escaping in the scrum.

I poked my head inside Willie's Saloon, and there she was, my favorite redheaded bartender, Krista. She was pulling shot glasses from underneath the bar and stacking them into a pyramid, like some presentation.

"Hey," I said, probably a little louder than I should have.

Krista and half the bar stopped what they were doing to look at me, this frantic man standing just inside the door. I didn't care.

"Mike?" she said. "What's going on?"

"Do you have a shotgun or a pistol or something behind the bar?"

"Do I what?"

"Never mind. Just stay here, Krista. Do not go out into the street for a while."

She looked at me like I was nuts, but as long as she did what I asked her to do, that was fine. She could think I was crazed, paranoid, or whatever.

After a moment, she nodded, and I backed out of the bar and let the door shut. I sprinted up Washington toward University Avenue, dodging college kids left and right. When I found a cluster of people too thick to navigate, I curved around Knoblock Street toward the Stonewall Tavern, not really sure where I was going or what I would do when I got there. Just had to put some distance between me and my apartment. Maybe I could attract the attention of these crackhead gangsters and lure them away from these crowded areas.

Across the street, on the campus side of Knoblock, I spotted Tanner in a long coat, despite the heat. Sweat beaded on his face. I'm sure he had Kevlar on underneath that jacket. His hand was inside the coat. I could see the tension on his face.

I squinted at the people around him. Saw four other faces I recognized, all of them members of the Sinaloa. All of them with hands on concealed weapons. On either side of the street were market-type booths and food trucks, funneling the pedestrian walkway into a much narrower space.

A choke point. That's why Tanner and the others were here. To squeeze our enemies through it and pick them off.

I studied the faces in the crowd ahead of me. The rednecks, the students, the school staff, the people from nearby towns. Almost every single one of them holding a signature Eskimo Joe's plastic cup frothing with watered-down Coors.

And then, dead ahead of me, saw five guys in the

crowd who had no Joe's cups. I recognized each of them as fitting the exact profile as others from the Tulsa gang. Sloppy clothes. Bags under their eyes. Shaved heads or crazy haircuts. Neck tattoos.

Walking shoulder to shoulder through the choke point, in my general direction.

One of them I specifically remembered from the failed trailer park bombing in Sand Springs. He'd shot at me, in fact. Tall guy, handlebar mustache curled around his mouth. I think he even might have been the same person who'd shot me in the ear.

If they saw me and started shooting, dozens of these pedestrians could take stray bullets. I ducked down and skirted to the left, pushing people out of my way. I could dart into the alley behind Qdoba and come out on the other side, and they'd never see me. Then I could double back around, get their attention and lead them away.

A gunshot blasted across the street. I popped up to see one of the Tulsa gang with a hand on his chest as blood oozed out between his fingers. And across the street, Tanner with his pistol out, barrel smoking.

Damn it. Too late now to lead them away.

Shots roared between the two groups and the night lit up with the electricity of gunfire and smoke. Pedestrians in the street took fire and collapsed to the ground. People screamed, ran in frantic circles. Exactly the pandemonium Ramón and Gus had wanted.

One of the gang members pivoted, and his eyes met mine. I saw the grin on his face as he swung his gun toward me. Between the two of us stood a skinny college girl in a tank top and cutoff shorts, frozen in place. Her hands were like claws at her side.

As the gang member closed one eye to aim down the sight of his pistol, I wrapped my arms around the girl's waist and tackled her to the ground. The shot rang out above our heads.

She screamed and punched me in the shoulder, wailing for me to let her go. I scrambled out from underneath her and ducked into the alley, then ran as fast as I could. I couldn't do anything useful out there. I wasn't about to pull out my Beretta and start indiscriminately blasting in the street.

I emptied out onto Maple, and by this time, most of the crowd had fled. Police sirens blared behind me. A man sprinted along the street with a turkey leg on a stick clutched in his hand.

I ran to West Street, back toward my apartment. I had to reach my car. By the time I'd returned to Washington and came barreling around the Plasma Donation building, I could barely breathe. My lungs burned. My head pounded. I'd forgotten all of my drunken injuries for a moment because they'd been replaced with the adrenaline of sheer panic.

I rounded the corner to my building and stopped short when I spotted a man sitting on the hood of my car. Wife beater t-shirt, ratty jeans with more holes than denim.

I didn't have time to evade. He lifted a pistol at me and pulled the trigger. His gun jammed. By the time he'd realized his mistake, I had my Beretta out. I put two in his stomach and one in his chest. The gun in my hand was like a barking pit bull.

I stomped over to him and grabbed him by the shoulder as he gagged on his own blood. He looked at me, desperate, probably realizing he was going to die in the next few seconds. Pleading with me.

I didn't care.

I yanked him off the hood of my car, jumped in the driver's seat, and screamed out of the parking lot.

PART III

THE CENTER OF THE UNIVERSE

CHAPTER TWENTY-FIVE

MY BACK ACHED from the janky Super 8 bed, but that didn't matter anymore. As the sun rose behind me, I sipped my coffee and stared at Gus' house through the gate. With my Beretta in my lap, I had everything I needed.

First, a bullet in Gus' forehead. Then, to the Freedom House to shoot Ramón in the balls. I would make him beg for his life, then force him to apologize for using me as bait to draw out the Tulsa gang, and especially for killing Pug. Force him to say the name Phillip Gillespie out loud before I emptied my clip into his stomach and waited for him to bleed out. Once he'd stopped convulsing, I'd reload and shoot Ramón in the head, just to be sure.

Forget whatever this did to my WitSec deal. I cared so little about it that I hadn't bothered to listen to the voicemail messages Delfino had been leaving for me. Yes, I knew El Lobo was supposed to arrive at OKC in about twenty-four hours. And I didn't care anymore.

I only hoped that I would still get the chance to testify, so the world would know the name Pug. They would know that he died for nothing at the hands of cruel men who got what they deserved, after the fact. Maybe in prison, I could create one of those memorial websites so I could see all of the nice things Pug's friends had to say about him.

I guzzled the coffee down to the grainy dregs and slipped the gun into my waistband, then exited my Jeep. A smear of blood still marked the hood from where I'd killed the guy in the wifebeater yesterday. I hadn't bothered to wipe it off when I'd finally settled on a motel last night. No one at the Super 8 had seemed to mind.

Someone had knocked on my room door at around midnight when I was halfway through my fifth of Jack Daniels. I'd ignored the knock until it went away. Feds, cartel, crackhead gang. The list of people in the world who didn't want to use me or kill me was rapidly shrinking.

I paused in front of Gus' gate and waved at the security camera. It emitted a little cybernetic whine as it swerved to track the movements of my hand. There was an intercom button on the brick pillar below it, but I didn't press anything. I knew they could see me.

Without any conversation, the gate buzzed and swung open.

It occurred to me that after I killed Gus, I should go into the house, find where the security tapes were kept, and erase them. And also that I didn't care if anyone saw me on a security tape or not.

I strode up to the house, feeling my underarms dampen from the already-stifling morning heat. Kept wiping my hands on my pants. I didn't want to have any issue gripping the gun, if necessary. I'd practiced a few times in the motel bathroom mirror this morning. Had felt jerky and slow. With surprise on my side, that wouldn't matter. I'd blow a hole in Gus' head before anyone could stop me, shitty reflexes or not.

I pounded on the door. Waited ten seconds, then pounded again.

The weighty door creaked open, and Gus' bodyguard Hank pushed his face through the crack. One of Hank's arms was in a sling. Probably had taken a bullet during the crackhead assault on Gus' house.

"Mike. I didn't expect to see you back here again. What do you want?"

"Can I talk to him?"

Hank shook his head. "He's not here."

"Come on, Hank. It's important. Just let me in."

"I'm not playing with you. Mr. Salazar is not at home right now. He left yesterday morning, and I have not seen him since."

"Where?"

Hank raised an eyebrow, a little suspicious. "He went out of town, and that's all I'm going to say."

I flexed my jaw, annoyed, confused, feeling empty.

He looked me up and down, with pursed lips. "You have blood stains on your shirt. Yours or someone else's?"

"Do you know when Gus is coming back?"

Hank shook his head again. "No, and I wouldn't tell you if I did. Get some sleep, Mike. You look like shit."

He disappeared back into the crack and the door shut behind him. I spun and slumped into a sit on the front porch.

What the hell was I supposed to do now?

CHAPTER TWENTY-SIX

I N HIGH SCHOOL, when I needed to go somewhere to think, I had a collection of favorite locations around Tulsa. The arboretum at Woodward Park. The swings at Haikey Creek Park. Under the bridge at 14th street. But none of them compared to the Center of the Universe when it came to finding a spot that gave you a sense of scenic change. It wasn't secluded. Far from it, actually, during the daytime. The Center of the Universe was a walkway bridge over some railroad tracks at the northern end of downtown Tulsa. In the middle of the walkway was a circle, and when you stood in it and spoke aloud, you could hear your voice echo in all directions. We'd always thought there was something different about this place.

After leaving Nichols Hills, I could have driven straight to Freedom House and put a bullet in Ramón, but Gus not being present had deflated my balloon. If I killed Ramón but Gus had a chance to slip away unharmed, it wouldn't be the victory I'd wanted.

No, not *victory*. That wasn't the right word. *Revenge* wasn't correct, either. Maybe *justice*. Justice for Pug.

While not quite clear-headed, it did occur to me that it wouldn't hurt to think the situation through before unleashing a hail of bullets in the name of justice.

So, I made the ninety-minute trek to Tulsa to feel the energy of sitting in the Center of the Universe for an hour or two. Don't get me wrong—I am not a believer in potions or magic crystals or the healing power of magnets. But, there *is* something about this place that you can't get anywhere else in the world.

As I sat in the Center of the Universe, I chatted with Boba Fett, listening to both of our voices bounce off the sides of the walkway. Business people with their briefcases and Bluetooth devices swerved to avoid crashing into me. Some of them scowled, but most paid me no mind, too wrapped up in their own meaningless lives to notice the grungy kid falling to pieces right there on the concrete. Going from one business meeting to another, thinking about their lake house mortgages and their investments and their country club membership dues.

"I just don't know why I should care," I said. "Even if I get justice, he's still gone."

It can get better, Boba said.

"That's what you keep saying."

You're looking for the wrong end result. If you kill Gus and Ramón, sure, you'll feel better. But only for a little while.

"You were the one telling me to kill them."

No, I never said that. You heard that. How about you win by surviving instead?

"Survive to do what?"

To live a new life as someone else. You can be anything you want to be. Do anything you want to do.

"Or, I could fail, and Ramón will put a bullet in me too. And just before he kills me, he'll make sure I know he won. My last thought will be how I messed up everything good in my life, and he gets to go on."

Or, you could quit being a baby. You still have time. How about you finish what you started and get Luis Velasquez on tape?

"I don't even know if that's possible."

Boba fell silent as the sounds of dress shoes and high heels clicked on the concrete bridge. From far away, a train rumbled along the tracks, coming closer.

My phone rang, and I flipped it out of my pocket and answered, without thinking.

"Michael?" Gus said.

"Gus?"

"I'm glad I caught you. I wasn't sure that you would be able to escape from the mess in Stillwater yesterday."

I gritted my teeth and resisted the urge to scream about how he'd created that mess by using me as bait. Instead, I inhaled an even breath and said, "I did escape."

"Good, good. I wanted you to know that despite what Ramón suspects, I know it was not you who stole the card from him. I meant it when I said I believed this matter to be settled."

I didn't know what to say. I could grab a little rush of adrenaline by blurting out, *no, it really was me, and his worthless business card is sitting on my kitchen counter right now. And my best friend is dead because of it, so I'm going to make you bleed until you beg for your life.*

Or, I could keep my mouth shut, and that's what I did. The train approached, a shrill whistle cutting through the air.

"I am going to Mexico for a few days," he said. "It cannot be avoided. Ramón will be coordinating El Lobo's visit tomorrow."

A flash of hope burned in my chest. I hadn't known for sure if Velasquez was still keeping the appointment, but now Gus had confirmed it.

"Okay," I said.

"He will need some help ensuring that the building is secure. Lobo insists that we sweep for government listening devices, fortify all entrances and exits, among other things. Please be available to assist him during the day."

Some douchebag in a three-piece suit who wasn't paying attention tripped over me, and I almost fumbled my phone. I cleared my throat and repositioned the phone against my ear. "Of course, Gus. Anything you need."

"Very well. I appreciate your loyalty and the sacrifices you have made, Michael. I will not forget it."

He ended the call, and I stared at my phone. El Lobo was going to be at the Freedom House. Tomorrow. I still didn't have a seat at the table, but I was going to be in the same building as him. I could still get close. All I needed was for him to speak within earshot of me. Maybe that would be good enough.

Maybe I could still make this happen.

And if not, I could always kill Ramón the day after.

CHAPTER TWENTY-SEVEN

MAYBE I SHOULDN'T have, but after spending so much of yesterday on the road, I returned to Stillwater so I could sleep in my own bed. And partially to stop by Willie's Saloon one last time to see Krista, but the bar was closed. Half the town had shut down because of the gang war in the streets. Such a thing was unheard of in tiny college towns like this. Eighteen dead, including five Sinaloa members, ten from the Tulsa gang, and three civilians who happened to be in the wrong place at the wrong time.

The gang war was over, or so I'd heard. The Tulsa gang couldn't withstand any more losses, and they had agreed to a sit-down, a week from now.

Tanner was missing, presumed to be among the dead. I wanted to hate him for snitching on me to

Ramón, but he was the one who'd warned me about the impending attack. I owed the kid my life. Since Pug's death had ripped my heart fully open, I didn't have any room to mourn for Tanner, but I did wish he hadn't been involved.

I blamed the Sinaloa for recruiting so young. I'd been too drunk to care about the organization I was joining. It had been Pug's idea, and back then, he hadn't known the extent of their power. We didn't even know it was a cartel until a year or so later. We were just making insane amounts of cash for delivering packages and driving people from one city to another. When you're young and swimming in money, it's easy to turn your ethical code into a sliding scale. Even so, we knew it wasn't right.

But Tanner had been too naive to know any better. Just a kid.

As I struggled to rise from my bed in the morning, the full weight of the day dawned on me. El Lobo would be here, in Oklahoma, in a few hours. I would have a maximum of one chance to get near him and make him admit something that I could give to the feds.

I cracked a beer to ease into the morning and stepped out onto the wooden walkway outside my apartment. The air felt strange; thick and humid. I smelled the impending rain, and the sky offered a hint of yellow tint within the blue, cloudless heavens.

Footsteps creaked up the stairs at the end of the

walkway. I set the beer on the ledge and hunkered down, ready to somersault back into my apartment if necessary. But, when the two heads of Agent Delfino and her male companion from the other day appeared, I relaxed, a little.

"Michael," Delfino said, "can we talk inside?"

I snatched my beer and returned to the apartment, giving them only a little flip of the hand as an acknowledgment.

I slumped into my Papasan chair as Delfino and the man entered and shut the door behind them. The unnamed agent wore a messenger bag slung over his shoulder.

I didn't offer them a seat.

"I heard about Pug," Delfino said. "I'm sorry. There's going to be a reckoning for what happened to him. I can promise you that."

I sipped at my beer and didn't answer. A reckoning. As in, *all debts get paid. The truth always comes out.*

I wondered if they were ever going to figure out about the cop I'd killed out at Lake Carl Blackwell. I hadn't bothered to check the news about him.

Delfino pointed at the man next to her as he removed his sunglasses. "This is Special Agent Vohlman. He's going to help you get ready today."

Vohlman lifted the messenger bag from his shoulders and set it on my carpet, knocking over a couple of empty beer bottles. He slid a hand inside the bag and withdrew a device that looked like a battery pack, and then a small microphone. Then, a length of thin cable.

When I realized what those things were, my heart pounded in my chest. My mouth went dry and the room tilted.

Vohlman held up the battery pack. "This goes down the back of your pants. There's a little latch here to attach it to your belt loop, but you'll need to wear a shirt long enough so that it won't show if you bend over."

"Is there any chance they'll search you today?" Delfino said.

I rolled my aching shoulders in a shrug. "They... they don't usually, but El Lobo hasn't ever visited before. I have no idea what today is going to be like."

"We can do this without the battery pack," she said, "but the range won't be as good. If you go somewhere with thick concrete, like a basement, we'll lose you. Radio interference, too."

Vohlman sucked his teeth for a second. "I'm thinking no battery pack. It's a big risk on such a volatile day. We recommend you also use your cellphone's voice recorder app as a backup, in case anything happens. Just turn it on and keep it in your pocket."

He opened a box sized for a wedding ring and handed me a tiny hearing aid. "Put this in. It's the only way we'll be able to communicate with you once you enter the building."

I accepted the hearing aid and pushed it into my ear.

Felt strange, like my head would naturally tilt with it in. I didn't like the pressure in my ear canal.

"Take your shirt off," Delfino said.

I stood and removed my shirt. Had a brief flash about Steven, the guy Ramón beat in the warehouse in Del City. Had he endured this same conversation with Delfino—or someone like her—a couple years ago? Had he been on the verge of shitting his pants, too?

I cleared my throat. "There was a guy who used to be one of us. Steven. I don't know his last name, but he escaped to Idaho. He got caught coming back into town to see his sick mom and Ramón caught him. Beat the snot out of him."

"What's your point?" Delfino said.

"Was he in Witness Protection?"

She shrugged. "Not that I'm aware of."

I hesitated, not sure if I should believe her.

Delfino frowned at me. "We're going to take good care of you."

"Where will you guys be?"

"In a van down the street. We'll have eyes on you while you're outside, but our in-building surveillance is limited."

She walked to me and placed the bug on the right side of my chest. "Whatever you do, don't take off your shirt. Wear a button-down, if you have one."

As she applied a piece of tape to hold the bug in

place, I grew woozy. My head swam and my knees wobbled.

Delfino paused. "You can do this, Michael."

My cheeks felt flushed and stars dotted my vision. "But what do I do? They said I wasn't allowed in the room with him. I can't just walk in there. I told you before: I'm not a big-shot. I'm just a guy. They won't let me near him."

"We had an idea about that," Vohlman said. He reached into the messenger bag and pulled out a little Ziploc baggie of white powder. Tossed it at me and I caught it.

"Say you have a present for him," Delfino said. "You walk in there with this Bolivian marching powder, everybody's going to be your best friend."

As I stared down at the meager baggie of coke, my eyes rolled back into my head, and that's the last thing I remember before I passed out.

CHAPTER TWENTY-EIGHT

AS I PARKED in the Freedom House parking lot, I realized the sky above me had turned an eerie shade of green. The air felt even thicker here than it had in Stillwater. My lungs had to work harder to push the muggy air in and out.

"Michael, you reading me?" squawked the piercing voice in my ear.

I flinched in my seat. "Shit, Delfino, yes. Turn it down, please, or you're going to bust my eardrums."

"Sorry," she said at a more reasonable volume. "Connection looks good from here. We're east of you, closer to Kelley Avenue. If you're in trouble, or you need anything, speak up."

"How do I do that?"

She paused. "A code word or phrase? Whatever you like."

I was going to suggest that I could barf to get their attention, but I wouldn't want to cry wolf too many times. "Sure. If I start talking about Oklahoma State football, I'm in trouble."

"Got it. We can be there in two minutes. I'm going to mostly stay out of it because I don't want to be a distraction. "

Too late for that, but I kept my mouth shut as I opened the car door. The humidity in the open air took my breath away. Like walking into a sprinkler.

I opened the front door of the Freedom House to find none of the usual halfway house residents inside. Maybe they'd all been cleared out for the day, taken on a field trip somewhere. Instead, I saw what remained of the Oklahoma City contingent of the Sinaloa cartel running around the hallways and rooms of the ground floor, frantic and panicked. Carrying trays of drinks and finger foods like it was some cocktail party. Guys I'd never seen before with large guns slung over their shoulders, opening closets and whispering into walkie-talkies.

I paused in the middle of the lobby, taking it all in. Conference room and manager's office along the wall to my left. Ahead of me, stairs up and a hallway to the kitchen. To my right, some closets, a door to an unused office, and the stairs down to the basement.

I had no idea where I was supposed to go or what to do next. The pressure of the poorly-fitted earpiece made my head thump. The bug duct taped to my rib cage felt like a tumor jutting out from my body. I wanted a drink.

One of the armed men I'd never seen before noticed me, and he leveled an AR-15 at my head. Looking down the sight at me, even though I was only fifteen feet away. He abandoned his spot next to the basement stairs and took a few deliberate steps toward me.

"Who are you?"

I tried to speak but the words caught in my throat. The guy wrapped his finger around the trigger. His shoulders clenched, and I got the sense that he was an inexperienced bodyguard. Maybe he'd let a stranger get too close to El Lobo before, and he'd rather shoot first than make that mistake again.

I showed him my empty palms. "No, it's cool. I'm—"

"He's okay," said a voice from behind me.

I spun to find Ramón glaring at me. "Where the hell have you been? I've been texting you all morning."

Ramón. I'd been distracted for part of the morning with all the procedural stuff. Now I remembered why I was really here. To see this grimy piece of shit go down for what he did. To see justice happen.

That is, if I didn't kill Ramón first. Still couldn't make up my mind about how I wanted the rest of this day to unfold.

If I'd had my Beretta on me, I might have revealed it and put a hole in Ramón's head before sprinting across the lobby to flee. Actually, I'd shoot him twice, just to be sure. That's probably why Delfino and Vohlman had insisted that I leave it back in Stillwater.

Ramón stormed over to me, and I focused very hard on not wrapping my hands around his throat. "My phone died," I said through clenched teeth.

"Phone died," he said. "Right. Anyway, it doesn't matter. I need you to go down to Moore."

"What?"

A power drill roared in my ear, and I angled my head to see some guy with a tool belt removing the doorknob from the conference room. They were changing the locks. Good to know.

Ramón snapped his fingers in front of my face. "Are you listening to me? You need to go visit the Italian chump at that bar in Moore. The guy with the limp, whatever his name is. You know who I'm talking about."

"You can't leave," Delfino said in my ear. Her voice took me by surprise, and I almost replied *I know, I know*, but I stopped myself at the last second.

"Why do I have to go?" I said.

Ramón frowned at me, then he pulled a roll of cash from his jeans and stuffed it in my shirt pocket. "He was robbed and needs some money. Go now, you can be back in an hour. We'll need your help around here with security."

"You can't send someone else?"

He sneered. "I'm sending you."

"But," I said, and before I could get any more words out, Ramón grabbed me by the shirt.

I panicked. If he pulled the buttons off my shirt, everyone in the room would see the bug taped to my chest. I let him pull me closer, trying to offer no resistance.

"Are you kidding me?" Ramón said. "What is wrong with you?"

"Nothing, Ramón. I'm fine."

"Then you go right now. Not another word. We need to keep this chump happy."

I nodded my surrender, and he released his grip on my shirt. As I walked past him and out the door, I listened to Delfino frantically sigh in my ear.

"Michael, what are you doing? You can't leave. Lobo might be gone in an hour."

"I don't have any choice," I said under my breath. "If I refuse his order he'll send me home or have me beaten at the warehouse until I've learned my lesson. I have to walk out this door."

When I stepped out into parking lot, the sky had inexplicably turned dark. Like going from noon to midnight in a flash. Above my head, I could see nothing but purple and charcoal clouds swarming with an unmistakable menace. A light breeze ruffled my hair and rain splatted the concrete around me.

"Did it suddenly turn into night time?"

"Big storm coming," Delfino said. "Tornado watch.

Michael, you can't leave the vicinity. You have to think of something and get back inside there."

"Give me a damn minute to actually think, and maybe I will," I said, and I wanted to rip the stupid communication thing out of my ear.

As I fished my car keys out of my pocket, three black SUVs rolled up and parked on the street. The passenger door of the middle one opened, and the other two stayed closed, tinted windows revealing nothing. Out stepped a man in a sharp black suit. He opened the rear door, and from it emerged the head honcho.

Luis Velasquez, AKA El Lobo. Dark aviator sunglasses, slicked-back hair. Without a little girl on a swing to push, he carried an air of malevolence about him. I could almost see him scowling behind those mirrored sunglasses.

This was the guy I was supposed to earn an audience with using a measly baggie of cocaine? *Hey dude, wanna get high?* That suddenly seemed like the most ridiculous thing I'd ever heard.

Lobo and his entourage made their way into the building. I, on the other hand, stood there, with nothing to say, nothing to do as my clothes were becoming heavy with the escalating rainfall.

I doubled back around the building and paused, leaning up against the brick exterior. Just me, the dumpsters, and the mewling tomcats. A warm rain began to fall in sideways sheets as the wind whipped against my face.

How the hell was I supposed to pull this off if Ramón wouldn't allow me in the building?

When I turned around, I found a .44 Magnum in my face. The arm holding it belonged to the pierced redneck from Sand Springs, the one who'd jumped into the river to avoid me.

CHAPTER TWENTY-NINE

PIERCED ONE SNEERED. "Thought you'd never see me again, didn't ya?"

"Michael?" Delfino said in my ear. "Who is that? Who's talking? We had to withdraw our camera drones because of the storm. Please tell me who you're talking to."

Pierced One smirked, rainwater drizzling into his mouth. "Cat got your tongue?"

His finger hovered over the trigger of his .44 as his chest heaved in and out. His mouth was open in a snarl, showing yellow and gray teeth. "Your friend killed my brother."

I had been the one to shoot his brother in the throat, but I wasn't going to argue the details.

I almost felt sorry for the kid. As much as I wanted to end Ramón, this pierced guy felt exactly the same about me. "Yeah, well, he's dead now too. Instant karma paid us all back for that one."

His head cocked to the side, and his eyebrows knitted together. I could see my comment about karma had confused him.

Another beat of silence passed. Had to do something.

I took my chance. I threw up a hand to knock his pistol to the side. The gun flew from his slippery grip. I heard it clatter to the ground, but didn't bother to watch where it had fallen.

I punched Pierced One in the gut, and he leaned forward, exposing his chin. I followed with an uppercut. He stumbled back, dazed, septum piercing swinging under his nose.

I advanced on him, and he spun, which surprised me. I raised my fists wide, expecting a right or left hook, but he surprised me again. Shot out a fist directly to my throat. He connected with my windpipe and for a moment, I couldn't breathe. The world dotted with stars.

I tried to yank in a breath, but it felt like someone had dumped glue down my throat. My eyes bulged out of their sockets.

He hunkered down, and I regained my wits and was able to draw a breath in time to swerve as his body blow missed me by a half an inch. I seized his outstretched hand and used his inertia to jerk him forward. As he moved, I slid to the side and then behind him while I angled his wrist. I pinned it against his back.

He tried to kick at my legs, so I pushed him face-first toward the ground. Applied more pressure on his wrist, hitching it up his back. When I was getting close to breaking his arm, he opened his mouth to scream, and I realized that I couldn't let the feds hear this.

I wrapped my free hand around his mouth, and he tried to bite at my fingers. He got my ring finger pretty good, and I reminded myself not to yelp.

"Everything okay?" Delfino said. "What's going on over there?"

I let go of Pierced One's wrist and slid my forearm underneath his neck, then I used my other hand to hold his head in place. "Everything is fine," I said, trying not to grunt as I squeezed. "Just give me a minute."

Pierced One squirmed, trying to buck me. In a few more seconds, his resistance blunted. It was working. I squeezed harder until he'd stopped fighting back altogether and I took my hands out from underneath him.

He collapsed onto the pavement, still alive, but unconscious. I'd never actually used a sleeper hold on someone before. I thought that only worked in the movies and professional wrestling.

Maybe I should have killed him then, but I didn't want to. I didn't need any more tangential deaths on my hands.

I flipped open the lid of the dumpster behind me,

then hefted Pierced One's limp body onto my shoulder. With a grunt, I dropped him in with the rotting food and shredded document debris.

"I'm sorry about your brother," I said. "But you're not the only person with problems."

"What?" Delfino barked in my ear. "What are those sounds? Who are you talking to?"

"No one."

"Doesn't matter. You have to get back in there."

I waited a few seconds until my breath had come back. "I know, damnit. But what do I do? I'm not supposed to be here."

"Think of something. Say you forgot to give your gift to El Lobo. When you pull out that baggie of coke, it's not going to matter."

I tensed my jaw, trying to stay calm. "That's not going to work. These people are not going to go all googly-eyed over an eightball."

"Then think of something else. Time is running out here, Michael."

I had to resist the urge to yank the earpiece out of my head. Delfino wasn't helping.

I hopped up the fire escape to the second floor and found myself outside the window of the same grumpy smoking woman from before, but didn't bother to knock. Based on the view downstairs, seemed like my employers had cleared everyone out for the day.

I looked back at the dumpster. Decided that it didn't

matter if he woke up or if someone found Pierced One. This would all be over in a few minutes, anyway.

I lifted the window and slipped inside to an empty room. After I had shut it behind me, the window rattled from the wind and rain outside. I hadn't seen a sudden storm this fierce since college.

My hand ran through my rain-slicked hair as I slumped on the bed for a minute. My chest heaved. This was all so surreal. How had this become my life?

"Michael?" said the voice in my ear, but it was garbled. I reached into my ear and plucked at the tiny little piece of wire to remove the earpiece. I flicked it a few times to dry it, then stuck it back in my ear.

"I'm here."

"What's going on inside there?"

"I just entered the second floor through the fire escape. Can you hear me? Your voice is all scratchy."

"Interference from the storm," she said, or at least, that's what I thought she'd said.

Didn't matter. I had more important things to worry about.

I crossed the bedroom and peered out into the living room. Nobody home. The front door was closed, and I leaned up against it, listening for sounds of motion in the hallway. With the rain and wind pelting the outside of the building, I couldn't hear squat over all the rabble.

So I opened the door and immediately caught a glimpse of a Desert Eagle shining under the hallway light, and a hand gripping the gun. I jerked back into the room. Heart racing. Head swimming.

Shit shit shit. Hallway guard. Why hadn't I expected that?

The kitchen was immediately to the right of the front door, so I ducked into it and crouched behind the dishwasher, which would shield me from view. Footsteps clomped inside, but I dared not peek. I focused all my energy on breathing quietly as the footsteps came to a stop. Waited five seconds for something to happen.

I eased my head around the corner of the dishwasher and saw a short man with his back to me. Gun in one hand. But what alarmed me more was that he was holding a walkie-talkie in the other. One call downstairs to Ramón and he could raise the alarm. Intruder in the building. Then they shuffle El Lobo out the front door, and my WitSec deal goes up in smoke.

Well, technically, I wasn't an intruder. I had every right to be in this building. But, if Ramón found out I was here and not on my way to Moore, he would go ballistic.

The man twisted the walkie in his hand, and I watched as his thumb pressed down on the *talk* button.

I reacted. Reached out and grabbed his ankle and I jerked it toward me. The walkie went flying from his hand as he slammed face-first into the carpet.

Before he had a chance to raise that Desert Eagle at

me, I punched him in the back of the head, then I flipped him over.

Out cold.

I recognized the guy.

"Sorry, Nando," I said. "It's nothing personal."

I took the gun from his limp hand and studied it. Was this Pug's gun? It looked just like the one he'd carried.

Didn't matter. I slipped it down the back of my pants. I probably should have grabbed a steak knife from the kitchen and slit his throat, but I couldn't do it. I liked Nando. He was one of the good ones. Nando had once taught me how to play this crazy card game named Egyptian Rat-Screw. Now, I'd bloodied his face and stolen his gun.

So, instead of killing him, I found some masking tape in the kitchen cabinet and wrapped his arms and legs, then his mouth and his eyes. Dragged him into the bedroom just as he was starting to stir.

My head buzzed with thoughts about what would happen if someone found him here. Nothing good, for sure. If Pierced One woke up and wandered into the building looking for me, someone would just shoot him and go back to business as usual. But one of our own guys trussed up like a kidnapping victim? That would raise some eyebrows.

And as I left him there, still with no idea how I was going to pull this off, I shut the door to the apartment behind me and crept down the hallway toward the stairs.

And that's when I experienced my first ray of hope.

Ramón's voice drifted from down the stairs, giving someone orders.

That meant he wasn't in the room with El Lobo. And that meant if I could find a way to skirt past Ramón and get in that room, I still had a chance.

CHAPTER THIRTY

I DIDN'T UNDERSTAND why, if Gustavo was out of town and Ramón wasn't in the meeting room, why El Lobo was even here in the first place. What was the point of all these local visits to Dallas and Oklahoma City and other places, anyway?

It didn't really matter. Whatever cartel business El Lobo had here, that didn't concern me. I had to get both him and me speaking on tape so the feds could match his voice to his face, and put me at the scene with him. Anything else that existed in the universe at this moment was not my problem.

As I crept down the hallway, inching closer to the stairs, I could almost make out what Ramón was saying. The wind and the rain outside screamed through the shoddy glass windows of this aging building.

"Go check the basement now," Ramón said. "I don't want to hear another word about it."

I thought I next heard footsteps, but couldn't tell for sure. The building felt like it was swaying a little under the strain of the weather. An old brick building like this might crumble to a pile of rubble if it rained hard enough. I'd always assumed that the asbestos fumes were the most dangerous thing in here. Never had it occurred to me that the building might collapse in on itself in the middle of a storm.

"Michael, what's going on in there?" said Delfino's garbled voice.

I dropped to my belly and inched toward the top of the stairs, trying to listen through the rain. Glanced down over the rim into the lobby to find the area free of people. That *had* been footsteps, and now Ramón and that anonymous order-taker had dispersed.

I stood and eased down the stairs, with my eyes on that conference room door. On the other side, El Lobo and unknown others were talking, making deals or plans or whatever.

I had to get in there.

"Michael, respond please," Delfino said.

I took the baggie of coke from my pocket and tossed it a couple inches into the air, letting it flop back onto my fingertips. I still didn't think being the Cocaine Gift-Bringer was a smart plan, but I didn't have anything else.

Maybe I could approach it as if I were going to give him the cocaine, but then I trip, and the baggie goes flying. I apologize, and he apologizes, and then we're both on the recording. Or, they shoot me in the head for interrupting the meeting and let my bleeding corpse stay sprawled on the floor until they're done talking about whatever it is they're talking about.

Maybe I could walk in there and tell them all that we needed to move to a different room because of the storm, or something like that. Maybe I could get some flashlights from the storage beforehand and try to pass them out. They probably wouldn't shoot me for being a Good Samaritan. Probably.

No, those were stupid ideas. I could always go with the simple *walked into the wrong room* tactic. Then, once I was in there, I could bust out that pathetic baggie of coke. Something to do while we waited. All I needed was Lobo saying a few words.

Out of time. Whatever I did, this had to happen. Now.

"Today's not my day," I said.

I reached out to open the conference room door. Before I could, a blaring alarm filled my ears and I stumbled back from the sound.

Tornado sirens. Not here. A mile or so away. Probably near the capitol building.

The conference room doors in front of me jerked open, and I saw six or seven men in slick suits inside, getting up from their seats. I didn't recognize any of them, but they all eyed me like I had an open wound on my head. They were cartel higher-ups, no doubt.

And then, emerging into my view, was the man himself, Luis Velasquez. El Lobo, the wolf. I was close enough to count all the gray threads in his wiry beard and the wrinkles around his eyes.

He glanced down at the baggie of coke in my hand and frowned.

"Lobo," I said, and it barely came out louder than a whisper.

To my left, the cutout windows on either side of the front door burst in a blistering fury. Glass shards cascaded onto the rug in front of the door.

Gunshots? Were the feds barging in now?

But I turned my head and saw no bullets slicing the air. What I did see through the open windows were swirls of trash whipping through the street. The darkness outside sliced every few seconds by flashes of lightning.

I turned back to El Lobo as someone grabbed him from behind and guided him into the lobby. *Basement, basement*, they were all shouting. All these men in their fancy suits, trundling through the lobby like cattle.

The men in suits ran past me, helping El Lobo down to the basement. All of them thundered down the stairs in waves. By the time I'd realized what had happened, the lobby was empty, and the basement door at the bottom of the stairs had locked behind them.

I was standing alone in the wind and crackles of thunder with a useless bag of cocaine in my hand.

I'd missed my chance.

CHAPTER THIRTY-ONE

"**D**AMN IT!" I SHOUTED, standing there in the lobby like an idiot. With the wind and the rain whipping through the busted-out windows, I could barely even hear myself.

"What?" Delfino said in my ear. "What's going on in there?"

"It's over. The meeting is over. El Lobo and everyone else have shut themselves in the basement because of the storm."

I wandered over to the front door to get a better look at the outside. Had to raise my hand to keep the rain from pelting my face. I'd been near tornados before, but hadn't ever felt a downpour this violent. It hurt as it smacked my palm.

"Please repeat," Delfino said. "Too much static. What was that about the basement?"

I peered out the broken glass of the window next to the front door and my eyes nearly bulged out of their sockets. A mile to the north, near the capitol building, was a cyclonic column of destruction. The outside had turned from midnight blue to gray, a swirling mass of wind and rain and bits of earth forming spinning wreckage.

A tornado, less than a couple minutes from here. If it came this way, everyone in this building would die, and there wasn't a damn thing I could do about it.

"Michael, can you still do this? If that twister comes any closer, we'll have to pull the plug."

My thoughts raced. I felt woozy. Needed action, now. No more theories, no more careful consideration.

El Lobo and the others were in the basement. Trapped down there. I was up here with a gun and free run of the building. What if I locked all the doors to keep everyone in? Then, I could shoot off the lock of the basement door, wave a gun in El Lobo's face, and demand he say his name into the microphone taped to my ribs. At gunpoint, he would have to do whatever I said. I might have to shoot all his bodyguards first, but I could make this work.

I had to make this work.

"I have a plan," I said, and dashed across the lobby to the closet across from the halfway house manager's office. Ripped back the door and frantically searched the inside. Chains, ropes, anything I could use to seal those doors from the outside.

I didn't find anything like that, but I did discover four untouched rolls of duct tape on a shelf at the top of the closet. I snatched all of them, sliding them up my wrist and onto my forearm for safe keeping. I had to hurry, because if that twister veered this way, the building really would collapse under the strain. If El Lobo died, I might as well die too.

I glanced back at the front door at those broken windows. Duct tape wasn't going to be enough to seal them. Shit. My throat had gone so dry that I couldn't swallow. A headache pounded behind my eyes, making the world thump like a bass drum.

I'd worry about that later. Close up the back and the side door first, then deal with the front door problem.

I raced along the hallway, through the kitchen, and to the back door. Stared at it for a second. If I went outside and taped the door shut, how would I get back in? And what about the windows? There were windows on the ground floor, and anyone wanting to escape could just shoot those out. Or they could scramble to the second floor and use the fire escapes.

Stupid idea. I wasn't thinking clearly. My brain had turned on me.

"Damn it," I said. "This isn't going to work."

"Say again, Michael," Delfino said. "I can't read you."

Time to switch to the straight-forward plan. I'd

shoot off the basement lock and hope that didn't give Lobo's bodyguards enough time to prepare for me. Maybe his guards would think it was the storm. Then I'd barge in. Kill anyone with a gun pointed at me. And then get Velasquez on tape, hopefully a few seconds before the cavalry arrived or before anyone fled past me.

"Get ready," I said to Delfino. "This is going to be over in a couple minutes."

I raced back through the kitchen to reach the stairs down to the basement. Thoughts in my brain swirled like bits of toilet paper circling the drain, faster and faster. I threw my shoulder into the swinging kitchen door and barreled down the hallway, not even looking.

When I reached the lobby, I finally looked up.

And saw Ramón, standing outside the manager's office twenty feet away, staring at me with his jaw dropped. His phone in one hand, a hammer in the other.

"What are you doing here?" he said. "I sent you down to Moore."

For a second, I didn't even register what he'd said because I was too busy staring over his shoulder. Through the broken window, I was watching the tornado tear into the duplexes on the other side of the street, flinging their roofs into the sky like a child tossing flowers into the air. The buildings crumbled as the tornado pushed through the collection of little homes. A solid black mass of chaos. At least I couldn't see any people flying through the air, limbs breaking from the force.

The wind and the rain howled through the blown-out windows like the ghastly screams of demons. We were all going to die in a few seconds, no matter what.

"Answer me," Ramón snarled.

I suddenly noticed that my asshole boss was standing on the opposite end of the lobby. Ramón was here, in the same room with me. The man who had murdered my best friend only a couple days ago.

He'd caught me. I couldn't talk my way out of this. Without thinking, I whipped my hand back to my waistband and tugged the Desert Eagle out. Lifted it to shoot.

For a big guy, Ramón was quick. My motion was too slow, and by the time I'd pulled the trigger, he'd already started to duck. The Desert Eagle roared in my grip, and the bullet sped across the room, blasting a chunk out of his shoulder. I'd aimed for his head.

Next thing I knew, something bit my hand.

I looked down to see Ramón's hammer knocking the pistol away from me and the hand cannon tumbling to the floor. My eyes followed it, and then the breath whooshed out of me as Ramón tackled me and drove me to the ground.

My head smacked against the floor, and my eyes rolled back into my head. Felt immediately groggy. My eyes fluttered for a few seconds, turning the world into a slideshow.

The gun had skittered across the carpet, ten feet away. But I couldn't move because Ramón was pressing his full weight down on me. He pinned my shoulders to the floor and scooted up on my chest, then drove his knees down on my arms to keep them in place.

He slugged me in the face with his left and then his right. My head swiveled as he punched me and my eyes filled with tears. I couldn't see, and then I couldn't breathe as his hands wrapped around my throat. Fingers sinking into my flesh. Pressure building.

"I should have done this a long time ago," he said through gritted teeth. His hands pressed tighter, and the compression made my head feel like it was going to pop.

His thumbs dug into my windpipe, and he was still ranting, but I couldn't hear it. Couldn't even hear the storm outside any longer. Spittle ejected from his lips as he growled and swore. His eyes burned like the sun. I could see the pores on his nose. His breath stank like rotten death. He pressed harder.

Squeezing the life from me.

I flashed back to the psycho cop doing the same thing. Wanting to end me. But Ramón didn't have a gun in a side holster to save the day.

And then, I felt myself slipping, falling, growing smaller. Folding inside myself as the dark space around me expanded, reaching infinity. I wanted to sleep. Let myself melt into nothingness. My eyes drifted to the front door, shaking on its hinges as the tornado ripped the outside street into tatters. Chunks of concrete sailed into the air and joined the scrum of the vortex.

I had a brief moment of hope that Delfino and her agents might burst through the door and pull Ramón off me, but that wasn't going to happen.

No one was coming to save me. I was going to die here, on this floor, right now.

CHAPTER THIRTY-TWO

AS I SLIPPED into unconsciousness, the front door of the Freedom House popped open under the weight of the storm. It thwacked against the blown-out inner windows, making more shards of glass crash to the floor.

Ramón briefly relaxed his hands. He turned his head for a moment, and that allowed me to take in a labored and painful breath.

His distraction only lasted for a half second, but the brief oxygen rush to my brain brought me back to the surface of consciousness. The blackness of the world faded and I could feel my body on the floor of this room.

I didn't want to die. I didn't have to die. I couldn't let myself die.

I tested my left arm as Ramón resumed squeezing,

but his knee had firmly pinned it to the floor. My right arm, though, could move a little. I wiggled it and made some room, using the duct tape rolls around my forearm as traction. The roundness of the rolls provided me a quarter inch of space I could use to maneuver. Once I'd gained a bit of leverage, I freed the arm. Jerked my shoulder back toward my head.

Ramón tilted to the side as my arm slipped out from underneath him, making his knee sink to the floor. He angled his head, confused, but that's all the time I gave him to collect himself.

My hand shot up between his legs, and I gripped his crotch with all of the ferocity I could muster in my barely-awakened state. I felt his testicles in my hand, and I squeezed, trying to rip them from his body.

He wailed and instinctively pulled back from me, releasing his grip on my neck and freeing my other arm. I let go of his nutsack and grabbed each of his wrists with my hands, then I twisted them, one on top of the other, and pushed to the right.

Off balance, he toppled like a rock onto the floor. Head smacked like dropping a basketball.

Still on my back, I rolled over and punched him in the face before he could get to his feet. Felt his nose crunch underneath my knuckles. As I pulled my hand back, a thin line of blood trailed after it.

I scrambled to my knees and cracked him with a left hook, then a right, then again, not giving him time to recover. My hands blurred from the movement, and his head whipped back and forth with each blow.

The windows inside the manager's office burst but the sounds were only twinkling memories. Something barely half-real.

I punched him until my hands were numb; until he was too dazed to put up his arms to block my blows. With each punch, his head became more and more like a rag doll, but I didn't stop. I wanted to pound his face into mush.

I pushed him onto his back and then straddled his chest. His shirt had ridden up, exposing a pocket knife on his belt loop. I snatched the knife and unfolded the blade, then held it to his throat.

"Wait," he said, his eyes barely open, his face a mass of bruised flesh. He tried to say more, but blood rushed into his mouth, and he gagged.

"No," I said. "I'll never wait for you again. I took your wolf card, not Pug. I stole it from you, and now Phillip Gillespie is dead because of it. He was a beautiful human being, and you're just a piece of shit and a bully. How does it make sense that you get to live, and he doesn't?"

"Please," he said, spitting blood and bile. "You don't have to do this."

True, I didn't have to do this. But I also realized that no matter what happened after this with me and Witness Protection and the feds and jail, I didn't want to hear another word out of this man's mouth for as long as I lived. I didn't have to.

I dragged the blade across his neck, opening it like cutting a raw steak.

He gurgled and gasped. His head vibrated, and his eyes bugged out as his hands flailed at his throat. I rose to my feet and took a step back, watching him desperately trying to close the hole in his throat. But it was too late. The puddle of blood around him turned into a pond.

And I loved it. For the first time in a long time, I felt a sense of accomplishment. A sense that I was doing something good for the world. Solving a problem. Snuffing an evil force.

In ten more seconds, he stopped flailing. His head lolled to the side, his eyes open. I removed all of the duct tape rolls from my forearm and dropped them on the floor next to Ramón's body.

"A reckoning," I said.

I couldn't bring Pug back, but I could do this, at least. I could make sure that Ramón would never hurt anyone, ever again. This had to be a plus in the universe's tally sheet.

"Michael?" Delfino's voice scratched in my ear. "Are you there? We're coming in to get you as soon as it's safe."

Oh shit. The feds were on their way, and I hadn't done any of the things I was supposed to do. I'd turned everything into a giant mess. I stared down at the dead body before me. Not only had I failed to get Lobo on tape, but I'd also murdered my boss in the lobby of a halfway house.

Murdered a person in cold blood.

There was no way out of this.

Before I could think of anything else, the front door of the lobby blew completely off its hinges and landed five feet from me. The building was shaking. Outside, the world had become a thrashing vortex of wind and rain and debris flying through the air.

I had to do something. Had to get rid of this body.

I snatched Ramón by the hands and dragged his corpse into the conference room, then shut the door behind me. It rattled on its hinges.

Panting, chest heaving, neck still throbbing from Ramón's grip. What was I supposed to do?

I tugged at the little piece of fishing line sticking out from the earpiece and yanked it from my ear. Tossed it onto the floor next to the dead body of the man who had terrorized both Pug and me for the last few years. Who would never terrorize anyone, ever again.

My eyes adjusted to the light in the room, and that's when it happened.

Amidst the chaos of the swirling mass of death engulfing the building, amid the turmoil of my oxygen-deprived brain barely able to connect thoughts together, my eyes landed on the conference table, at a single cell phone sitting there in front of a chair.

I wandered over to the table and reached out to grab the phone. Ramón's blood all over both of my hands. The screen was dark, so I pressed the home button to turn on the phone.

The screen lit up. The wallpaper on the phone showed a little girl, not more than five or six years old. Brown skin, dark hair. Hispanic. Eyes as black as marbles. Big grin on her face showing half a set of teeth.

I knew this kid.

I blinked, and it came to me. I'd seen this girl on a swing set in Plano, giggling as her daddy pushed her higher and higher.

This phone belonged to El Lobo.

He must have left it here in the pandemonium to escape to the basement.

This was it. My way out.

My shaking hand closed around the phone and I slipped it into my pocket.

CHAPTER THIRTY-THREE

WITH LUIS VELASQUEZ'S phone in my pocket, I stumbled back out into the lobby, confronted with the darkened circle of Ramón's blood in the middle of the room. The adrenaline was already starting to wear off. Maybe I'd been defending myself, but I had relished the feeling of slitting his throat open and watching him die. I dimly remembered the sensation of my dick growing hard in my jeans as I'd watched the life drain out of him.

I stared down at my hands. Blood lining the grooves of my palms like strands of silty rivers seen from a passing helicopter.

Somehow, while I hadn't been paying attention, I'd turned into a monster myself. No wonder my family hadn't spoken to me in years. No wonder I couldn't look at myself in the mirror without pouring a half-dozen drinks down my throat first.

I'd killed a police officer a little more than a week ago. And my life had been so insane since that night, I'd barely even thought about him at all in the last few days.

How did I become this? What did these people do to me?

For some strange reason, Krista the bartender popped into my head. What would she say if she could see me right now, broken and defeated, literal blood on my hands?

Oh, Michael McBriar? He's not boyfriend material. A crazy drunk who I flirted with for fun, for the element of danger.

I sat, lungs heaving. Wanted a drink. I needed a drink more than anything in the world right now. But I also knew that alcohol was not going to help. I'd used it as a crutch for all these years to escape from reality. Couldn't lie to myself about that any longer.

I looked out the front door and realized that the tornado had moved on. Evaporated. The sky was now a shade of charcoal tinted with green hues.

I got to my feet and floated out the front door. Rain still wafted in sheets, but the wind had left. Little chunks of black things like thin cow patties were everywhere. I stared at one for a second until I realized it was part of the roof. The duplexes across the street had been demolished, nothing but piles of concrete and steel and stone. The office park next to the duplexes, however, was completely untouched. Like new.

A force of evil so selective that it could erase one thing and ignore another thing separated by a few measly feet.

"Michael," Delfino said, but in real life this time, not in my ear. I looked left and right, found her hustling into my view from around the building. She was wearing a dark green raincoat, her hair plastered to her head. Panting.

She stopped her jog next to me and pointed at my hands. "You okay? You're bleeding."

"I don't know what happened to me." At that moment, I couldn't remember how I'd gotten that blood on my hands. I didn't think it was my blood. I had a dim memory of being shot at near a trailer park, one of the bullets tearing a small flap of flesh from my ear. No, that couldn't be the same blood. That had been days ago.

"We didn't get most of the audio," she said. "The storm fried all the equipment to hell. Did you get him on tape? Maybe recorded him with your phone?"

El Lobo. I was supposed to record El Lobo. "I didn't have a chance." I turned back to the house and pointed into the lobby. "He's right in there, though. He's down in the basement."

"No, he's not. He and his people left out the cellar door before the tornado hit this block."

I'd completely forgotten that the basement had its own door that led out the back of the building. "What? You let him go?"

"Of course we did, Michael."

All the cars with the tinted windows that had been parked on the street were now gone. I couldn't believe it. "All this, and you didn't even arrest him?"

"We don't have enough evidence to bring him in yet." She pointed a finger in my chest. "That was partly your job."

A pulse of despair threatened to engulf me. So much blood spilled, so much anguish, and it had all been for nothing.

"But he was here," I said.

"We've heard he's on his way to Little Rock next. So that's where I'm going."

"Wait," I said. "I don't have his voice on tape, but what if I had something else?"

"Like what?"

I reached into my pocket and removed the phone. Pressed the home button to wake the screen. I could practically see Delfino salivating.

"Is that his phone?" she said as she opened her palm.

I slapped the phone into her hand. "It is. Now, I want my damn WitSec deal."

Micah shifted on the couch, the shoebox full of memories of his past as Michael McBriar in his lap. The old love letters, the two thumb drives from Pug, the business card with the raised image of the wolf's head. The things he should have turned over as evidence. The things he'd been prohibited from keeping from his old life that he'd smuggled into his new life.

"That's it," Micah said. "I'm done. After that was the trial, my little stint in prison, coming here, floundering for a while, eventually getting sober. You know the broad strokes of the rest of it."

Frank sat back in his chair on the other side of the coffee table, rubbing a hand underneath his chin. "So, getting him on tape didn't even matter?"

"They said it would have helped, but Velasquez had so much damning information on his cell phone that it wasn't necessary. It linked him to everyone else in the organization. Emails and texts the government hadn't been able to access remotely, right at their fingertips."

"Wow, kid. You brought down a Mexican drug cartel. Can I just acknowledge how amazing that is?"

"Thank you, but I didn't. Not really. I mean, they still exist. They're not as powerful as they were, though."

Frank coughed into a handkerchief. "And the trial?"

"All I basically had to do was testify that I was the one who'd discovered the phone, and then I named all the names of everyone else I knew inside the cartel. After that, it was like dominos."

"I'm sorry about your friend. I didn't know how much he meant to you."

Micah traced the lines of the shoebox with his fingertips. "Thank you. Sometimes you go months or years without seeing someone, and it's no big deal, but the prospect of never being able to see a person again? It's a whole different thing."

"What about his land out there? His family land back in Oklahoma with the secret letters from Abraham Lincoln?"

Micah shrugged. "I'm not sure. It sold eventually, to someone. I never actually believed that junk about the buried treasure. I'm not sure if Pug believed it either.

Sometimes I think it was something he told himself so he could keep going. Give himself a reason to get out of bed."

"Either way, maybe someday you can buy the land back. Turn it into a nature preserve, or whatever Pug might have liked."

Micah winced as tears formed at the edges of his eyes. "I don't know if he would have turned it into a nature preserve, but I get what you're saying."

Frank nodded and folded his hands in his lap. Silence blossomed in the room. Micah wallowed in the overwhelming exhaustion of having spilled his life story. So many secrets now, out in the world. He didn't know how to feel, other than drained.

Micah took a breath, his lip trembling. "Am I a bad person?"

Frank shook his head. "No, kid. You did some bad things. It's not the same. Now that you're sober, you can take all that energy and put it into something good. Make the world better."

Micah opened the shoebox and sifted through photos until he found the picture of him and Pug standing near the canal at Bricktown in Oklahoma City. Some stranger had snapped the photo three days before they'd gone to Mannford, when Micah had smashed in the face of that pedophile. The day everything had changed. The beginning of the end.

When he lifted the picture, the black and white wolf business card was sitting underneath it. Frank leaned forward and nodded at the card. "You kept it?"

"I know I should have turned it over to the feds, but once I had my deal, I wasn't in the cooperative mood. In some ways, I thought I was honoring Pug by keeping it. I mean, he died because of this."

Frank nodded, said nothing.

"I miss him," Micah said.

"You always will. That doesn't go away. But it does hurt less often, and not as harshly as it does at first. It's been a couple years now, you're probably already seeing a difference."

Micah closed the shoebox and set it on the coffee table. "So, this 'making the world a better place' stuff? How do I do that?"

"First," Frank said, hooking a thumb at the pages of Micah's fourth step, sitting behind them on the kitchen table, "we're going to take those pages of your written inventory and burn them in your bathtub. All that crap is gone. From this day on, you're a new man. You're Micah Reed, skip tracer, sober person, son, brother, a student of the universe."

"Student of the universe," Micah mused. "First day of the rest of my life?"

Frank grinned. "Sure, if you like."

Micah stood and collected the pages from the table. The account of his past. He then dug around in a kitchen drawer for a book of matches and held the two objects in his hands. Found himself smiling, thinking what a pleasure it would be to set fire to the past.

If you enjoyed this book, please click here to leave a review.

NOTE TO READERS

Want to know when the next book is coming out? Join my reader group at www.jimheskett.com to get updates and free stuff!

Breaking Bullets is the first Micah Reed book set in my native Oklahoma. It was fun to write about places I knew growing up; to virtually revisit all those old haunts like the Center of the Universe in Tulsa. Plus, after months of emails from fans, I am now finally able to deliver more about Micah's backstory, and who he was before he took on that name. More to come on that later...

This is also the first Micah Reed book to feature first-person point-of-view from Micah. I thought it was necessary to get inside his head to help understand him as he experiences the events of the book; this novel features Micah doing a lot of bad things. He hurts people. I felt like first person POV would help the reader understand his motivations better. These insights into Micah's past and his thoughts help round out all we think we know about this mysterious man formerly named Michael McBriar. But, stay tuned, there are more insights coming...

If you started reading Micah Reed's adventure with this book, go back and take a look at Airbag Scars. Micah's backstory will make a lot more sense, and you can get this full length novel FOR FREE. It's not available for sale anywhere.

With that out of the way, thank you for reading my book!

Please consider leaving reviews on Goodreads and wherever else you purchased this book (links at www.jimheskett.com/breaking). It takes only a few seconds, and you have no idea how much it will help the success of this book and my ability to write future books. That, sharing it on social media, and telling other people to read it.

Are you interested in joining a community of Jim Heskett fiction fans? Discuss the books with other

people, including the author! Join for free at
www.jimheskett.com/bookophile

I have a website where you can learn more about me
and my other projects. Check me out at
www.jimheskett.com
and sign up for my mailing list so you can stay informed
on the latest news. You'll even get some freebies for
signing up. You like free stuff, right?

For Adam and Erik, two friends who left this world entirely too soon. It's an insidious disease.

Published by Royal Arch Books

Www.RoyalArchBooks.com

Please consider leaving a review once you have finished this book.
Want to know when the next book is coming out?
Join my mailing list to get updates and free stuff!

A NOTE ON CHRONOLOGY

While the Micah Reed novels are essentially standalone stories, each one does build on some elements from previous books. To see the list of how each story fits on the overall timeline, visit jimheskett.com/timeline. If you want to read them in order, check out that link.

ABOUT THE AUTHOR

Jim Heskett was born in the wilds of Oklahoma, raised by a pack of wolves with a station wagon and a membership card to the local public swimming pool. Just like the man in the John Denver song, he moved to Colorado in the summer of his 27th year, and never looked back. Aside from an extended break traveling the world, he hasn't let the Flatirons mountains out of his sight.

He fell in love with writing at the age of fourteen with a copy of Stephen King's The Shining. Poetry became his first outlet for teen angst, then later some terrible screenplays, and eventually short and long fiction. In between, he worked a few careers that never quite tickled his creative toes, and hasn't ever forgotten about Stephen King. You can find him currently huddled over a laptop in an undisclosed location in Colorado, dreaming up ways to kill beloved characters.

He blogs at his own site and occasionally podcasts about this and that. You can also scour the internet to find the occasional guest post or podcast appearance. A curated list of media appearances can be found at www.jimheskett.com/media. He believes the huckleberry is the king of berries and refuses to be persuaded in any other direction.

If you'd like to ask a question or just to say hi, stop by the About page and fill out my contact form.

More Info:
www.jimheskett.com

Made in the USA
Lexington, KY
04 June 2019